Bali with the Billionaire

Alexia Adams

Copyright

Bali with the Billionaire

By Alexia Adams
Copyright 2019 by Alexia Adams

Published by:
Alexia Adams
Suite 377
255 Newport Drive
Port Moody, BC V3H 5H1
Canada

Contact: Alexia@alexia-adams.com
www.alexia-adams.com

Edited by Brenda Chin and Amanda Bidnall, PhD

Ebook ISBN 978-0-9939126-9-6
Print ISBN 978-1-9991756-6-5

First Ebook Edition June 2019
First Print Edition September 2020
Product of Canada

Chapter One

Jade Irvine smiled as she took in the refined elegance of the hotel lobby. It was definitely an upgrade from where she normally stayed when working in Bali. Except she wasn't working until tomorrow. Right now, she was on a hen weekend with her three best friends. And they'd be well on their way to partying on if Jules wasn't having a "no, you hang up" Skype conversation with her boyfriend back in Australia.

"Oh, my God! Is that Henry Golding?" Lauren's high-pitched question had Jade, Karly, and a few other women scouting their surroundings. A giggle welled in Jade's throat. They probably looked like meercats to anyone who hadn't heard Lauren's question.

"Where?" Karly asked.

"Over there." Lauren nodded her head rather dramatically to the left.

The three friends peered into the hotel bar. A lone man sat apart from everyone else, his index finger circling the rim of the glass in front of him. Unfortunately, it wasn't a gorgeous actor needing a little cheer from four women celebrating an upcoming wedding. Still, he looked familiar…

"Actually, that guy's way hotter than Henry," Lauren—a self-professed expert on the male hotness scale—declared. "Is he a local? Jade, do you recognize him?"

She shook her head, still trying to place him. If they'd met in person, she'd never have forgotten him. She searched his features. "He looks sad," she said. "No one should be miserable in Bali. We should invite him to join us."

"Jade…" Karly and Lauren said in unison, warning tones in their voices.

"What?" she asked, flipping her long, dark hair over her shoulder, ready to go into action.

"We came to Bali to party before Karly voluntarily puts a noose around her neck," Lauren said. "Not so you can play Dr. Phil with a perfect stranger."

"It's a wedding ring, not a noose," Karly interrupted. The first of their tight-knit group to marry, she was ever ready to defend her decision to tie herself for life to one man.

Jade ignored the green-eyed monster whispering in her ear. If Keith hadn't been a lying bastard with a gangrenous heart, would she be as blindly hopeful heading toward the altar? Her eyes were automatically drawn back to the man at the bar. What was his story? Had his heart been shattered by a deceitful lover as well?

"I'm not playing Dr. Phil. But you have to admit he looks … lonely," Jade replied.

"He's not a koi fish that needs rescuing. Anyway, a guy that hot won't be lonely for long," Lauren said. As they watched, a scantily-clad woman approached the man.

"What'd I miss?" Jules asked as she arrived, her face all flushed. The Skype call must have gotten steamy before one of them came to their senses and hung up. "I thought we were going to Sky Garden. Are we having a starter drink here?"

They were the pick'n'mix of women. Karly, the bride-to-be, was blonde haired and blue eyed with the face of an angel and a laugh that made men hard. Jules had brown hair and eyes, and legs that went on forever. Lauren was the group's redheaded, hazel-eyed beauty with a legendary temper. But she was as fiercely loyal as rescue dog. Wherever they went, they attracted male attention.

Karly exhaled a melodramatic sigh. "Jade wants to fix the guy at the bar."

"I don't want to *fix* him," Jade said, while Jules asked, "What guy?"

They all turned back to the magnificent specimen who was once again alone. The woman who had tried to talk to him earlier was now chatting on one of the sofas with a balding guy dressed in shorts and a flower-print shirt. It seemed someone was working tonight.

"See, he's alone again," Jade said, unable to take her eyes from the man. There was something about him that called to her.

He reached into the pocket of his suit jacket and pulled out a phone, giving the screen a long glance before he answered. Rotating in his seat, probably to hear better, he now faced them full-on. His eyes were distant, as though concentrating on the voice on the other end. But his countenance didn't light with joy as it would if he was speaking with a loved one.

"Do not get involved, Jade." Karly put her hands on her hips like some 1950s housewife scolding her child for tracking mud onto the freshly washed linoleum. Karly was always trying, mostly unsuccessfully, to mother the other girls.

"But—"

"Remember the cake," Lauren said.

"Come on. You cannot compare that man to a birthday cake," Jade protested.

"It was your idea that nearly burnt down the school," Lauren continued. "You just *had* to make a cake for the gardener, even though we weren't allowed in the kitchen and none of us had the slightest idea what we were doing."

"His mother had just died. No one else was going to give him a cake." And *she* wasn't the one who'd left the tea towel near the lit burner. Although it was her idea to cook the cake on the stovetop. With her culinary inexperience, she'd figured it had to be way faster than baking it in the oven.

"And the filing fiasco?" Jules added, unhelpfully.

Jade huffed. "I don't appreciate you bringing up all my minor mishaps."

"Mrs. Kiddy lost an entire year's lesson plans and the manuscript she'd been working on for five years. It was hardly a minor mishap." Karly raised her hand as Jade was about to interrupt. "I know your intentions were good. Yes, she was stressed and couldn't find anything on her messy desk, but sometimes, sweetie, you do more harm than good when you help." Karly put air quotes around the last word, eliciting a snort of laughter from Jules.

"My favorite Jade misadventure was the bubble tsunami," Lauren added, like they were competing for the best disaster story.

The three other women dissolved into laughter. Karly wiped her cheeks as a few tears fell. "Only our Jade would have replaced the liquid laundry soap with bubble mix so the housekeeper's job wouldn't be so boring."

"There is no proof I did that," Jade said. Although she had. The poor woman had needed something to brighten her day. At least by then Jade had learned to cover her tracks in case things went sideways, as they inevitably did.

But this was different. The guy at the bar was a grown man. What harm could there be in inviting him for a drink and maybe a dance? "I still think we should ask him."

The four women peered into the bar again. The subject under discussion had completed his phone call and once more stared morosely into his drink.

"For once, I agree with Jade. I vote we bring him with us," Jules said.

For once, my arse. None of you girls need any convincing to follow me into trouble.

"You already have a boyfriend," Lauren reminded Jules.

"Yeah, but Sad-Man can watch our drinks while we get our groove on," Jules said. "Anyway, I was thinking maybe you could do with the company, Loly. It's been a while…"

Lauren made a face at Jules. "I'm focusing on my career at the moment, thank you very much. Besides, what about Jade? She's unattached as well."

All three friends turned pitying eyes on her. "Jade's still in recovery," Karly said quietly, like they were discussing a potentially fatal diagnosis at the bedside of an unconscious relative.

Jade squared her shoulders. "I'm not in recovery. I'm over the scumbag. But for the record, I'm not looking for love, just a good time."

"A guy that hot… I'd put money on him being a good time," Lauren said with a nod toward the man at the bar.

Jade moved a little closer to the entryway to get a better view. "Crikey. Now I know why he looks familiar. I think that's my boss for the week."

"You're going to translate for *him*?" Karly asked. "Good luck with that. I doubt I'd even be able to speak English standing next to him."

Jade shrugged, feigning a bravado she definitely didn't feel. After years of faking it, though, few could tell the difference. "It's a tough job. But someone has to do it. Watch my back, ladies, I'm going in."

Her friends laughed as she strode into the bar to introduce herself. What were the chances she could manage it without saying something inappropriate?

***

Harrison Mackenzie sipped his scotch and glanced around the bar. This upscale Indonesian hotel had managed to combine the local architecture with western touches so a traveler felt both at home and on holiday. Dark teakwood furniture was lightened with bright blue and red cushions. Tropical plants overflowed stone pots decorated with intricate Balinese carvings. Chrome lights and shiny glass surfaces gave a modern edge to the place. But not even the ever-swirling ceiling fans could dissipate the salty essence of the sea and the smell of coconut-scented sunscreen.

Too bad he wasn't on vacation. Although this was the last place he'd go to get away. Beaches and wild nightlife didn't appeal. He'd rather spend his off-work hours reading about ancient history. If he were to go abroad, it would be to an archaeological dig or someplace like Machu Picchu. He wouldn't hang out in a place known for the wild partying of its tourists. How the locals coped with the clash of cultures, he couldn't fathom.

"I could have gone in your place." Caleb's distant voice brought Harrison back to the phone conversation. "I know how tough Monday's date is for you." His friend must have forgotten that by crossing the date line, Harrison's Monday was tomorrow.

"It's fine. I'm fine. I … needed to get away this year."

Long pause. It could have been a problem with the connection from Canada, or maybe Caleb was figuring out what to say. "All right. But if you need me, I can be on the next plane out," Caleb said.

As if Harrison was going to ask his friend to hold his hand while Caleb's pregnant wife waited at home. He wasn't that selfish. Besides, marriage may have made his friend more open about his emotions, but that didn't mean Harrison was going to jump on that itchy hayride. As long as he didn't let himself feel, everything would be okay.

Convincing Malee to marry him was the best negotiation Caleb had ever concluded. She was perfect for him, and his friend and business partner had never been happier. But sometimes Harrison longed for the time when the deepest thing Caleb said was, "Want another drink?" Not everyone got a happy ending to their story.

"I appreciate the support," Harrison answered. "Give my love to Malee."

"Will do."

Harrison toyed with the idea of turning off his phone to avoid more awkward calls, more people asking how he was doing. But considering his father's precarious health, he kept it on.

He barely had the device back in his pocket before another woman sauntered over to him. Her long ebony hair fell nearly to her waist. Well-rounded hips swayed in a provocative movement that struck a resonating tune within his body. The black dress she wore would give a thirteen-year-old boy wet dreams if he saw it on a hanger, never mind on this woman, with generous curves in all the right places. It didn't leave much to the imagination, except perhaps which sexual position to start with. She was everything he despised himself for wanting.

Without even a pause, she perched her gorgeous ass on the stool next to his, swinging a strappy-high-heel clad foot so it almost brushed his calf. Up close, he could see that her eyes, which he'd expected to be dark like the rest of her coloring, were in fact deep green: pools of liquid emerald that lured him to forget the promises he'd made and drown in the desire she provoked. He shook his head to restart his brain, and her burgundy-stained lips parted in silent amusement.

"Are you waiting for your wife or girlfriend?" she asked without introducing herself. The middle finger of one hand was tightly pressed to the thumb, as though she'd been mid-meditation when she decided to proposition him.

"No, I have neither. I also don't pay for sex." Might as well move this encounter along so he could get back to nursing his whisky and going over his game plan for tomorrow's meetings. This was the first project to hit a snag since he'd become full partner in Caleb's investment firm. No way was he going to be bested by a painted design on a fricking T-shirt.

"Good to know. Have you ever had sex—free or otherwise?" The woman's Australian accent was a surprise. Until she'd opened her mouth, he'd pegged her for a local.

She flipped her hair over her shoulder and Harrison's eyes were drawn to the long column of her neck. What sensuous delights would he experience as he tasted his way from her lips to her ear and then down her lightly tanned skin to the collarbone so prominently displayed? Not to mention her glorious breasts, pushed to the top of her dress as though just waiting for an opportunity to escape the confines of the black silk fabric.

"Why do you ask that?" He could feel himself rising to her bait, a floundering sucker about to be enticed to his doom. *Never again.* Marshaling his inner iceman, he allowed his gaze to roam over her body before meeting her eyes with cool detachment—a look he'd perfected after years as a corporate lawyer. The expression told his competitors they were about to lose everything.

"You're so buttoned up. For God's sake, you're wearing a tie at a beach resort." She slid one black-polished fingernail down his blue-striped tie. He held his breath, praying the thing didn't catch fire. For a brief second, the urge to throw her over his shoulder and carry her upstairs to his suite flooded through him. But Harrison Mackenzie didn't lose control. Not anymore.

"I'm here on business."

She glanced around at the other patrons. Not one wore a suit, never mind a tie. "I hate to break it to you, mate, but there's no one here to do business with."

"And you're not working?" He raised an eyebrow.

Her husky laugh enveloped him as she slid off her stool, putting her within inches of his body. He breathed in the scent of some exotic flower with a hint of ginger and lemongrass. Damn the hunger that gnawed at him.

"Nope. Not tonight, at least. I'm here to have fun. Besides, you can't put a price on this body."

He had to agree with her there.

"Enjoy your business," she said, her husky voice laced with humor. Before his brain could come up with a suitable response, she glided away, ignoring the ribald comments of a group of men drinking in the corner. He'd noticed them earlier, waving their money around and propositioning any woman who walked near. Harrison was perversely glad when his mystery woman kept walking. He'd hate to risk a tear in his suit jacket having to rescue her from their loutish behavior. Although given her confidence, she could probably defend herself.

At the door, she glanced back at him once more, and he quickly turned away, annoyed that she'd caught him staring. Now he could get back to rehearsing his pitch for tomorrow. If it were a trial or contract negotiation, he'd be sure of his tactics. He knew exactly what he'd demand and where he could compromise.

This meeting, however, was different. He'd have to cajole and offer incentives to get the project back on track, find a way to get the other party to want to do more without offering much in return. The venture was already bordering zero net, and they didn't have time to move to another manufacturer if they were going to meet their pre-sales commitments. Plus, the whole discussion would be in Indonesian, and he'd have to rely on a translator to convey not only his words but his meaning, without revealing his desperation.

Giving up his legal career had been a no-brainer when he got to choose start-ups to fund and see through to IPO. It was exactly the kind of challenge he needed to forget everything he'd lost. Work was the one area of his life where he was now free to follow his passions. It would have to suffice.

He slung the rest of his whisky down his throat and made his way through to the lobby. His eyes searched for the woman in the black dress who'd talked to him in the bar, while his brain tried to reason that it would be better if he never saw her again. She was bold and brash and the exact opposite of everything his wife had been.

He shouldn't want to see her again—or run his fingers through her ink-black hair while he tasted her full lips.

But he did. *Damn it.*

Chapter Two

Jade ran damp palms down her most conservative gray dress and glanced into the mirror across the hallway to ensure her hair was still neatly tucked into a low chignon. She looked like a tax auditor. Or a high-priced lawyer about to rain down a legal shitstorm on some poor unsuspecting bastard. But the dour outfit clashed with the devilish twinkle in her eyes. How would her new boss react when the woman he'd assumed to be a prostitute showed up as his translator for the next week?

The logical side of her didn't blame him. After all, she had been dressed provocatively for her best friend's hen night—or hen weekend, as it had turned out. When the girls had heard that Jade was off to Bali on assignment, it had seemed like the perfect pre-wedding getaway.

So Karly, Jules, and Lauren had all booked flights to the Indonesian island, and the four of them had partied all night and recovered on the beach each day. When she'd approached Harrison last night in the bar, she'd forgotten that she was dressed to undress.

And then she'd flubbed it all and asked him if he'd ever had sex. Any chance he wouldn't remember that bit? Not likely. But he'd made his own gaffe, so maybe he wouldn't mention it.

If she hadn't been so stunned by her new boss in the flesh, he might have been sporting a black eye this morning for his assumption that she was a sex worker. The head shot on his corporate website had in no way prepared her for the whole awesome package that was Harrison Mackenzie. It gave no clue that his shoulders spanned two time zones, or that he filled a suit so well she wanted to rip it from his body and see all those glorious muscles for herself. Maybe he played ice hockey in his spare time. She'd heard those guys were built. Of course, it could all be padding. Perhaps he had the physique of a flag pole and a really great tailor?

Worst of all, his black-and-white web photo failed to reveal that he had blue eyes. Like, bloody-lose-your-mind-and-drown-in-them-blue. With his straight black hair and wide cheekbones, she'd expected dark eyes. He didn't seem like the type of man to give into the vanity of colored contacts, unless it was to disguise the haunting sadness that seemed to surround him.

It was odd. When he spoke, all that came across was stuck-up businessman. What if the pole-up-his-arse posture was a defense, kind of like her over-the-top confidence?

Dammit, were the girls right? Did she always want to *fix* people? Or was it, as Karly had once told her, just a reflex to avoid looking under her own bonnet?

Whatever. She was here to work—and work was one area of her life where no faking or repair was required. She could translate in her sleep if required, and probably did. Aside from her delicious boss, this assignment sounded like a snooze-fest. According to the itinerary, later this afternoon they'd visit the plant where a specialized paint product was being manufactured. She'd done her homework and familiarized herself with all the specific terminology in both English and Indonesian that she'd likely encounter.

What was a billionaire doing mucking about with paints and T-shirts? Maybe he was a closet craftie. The mental image of Harrison with his hands covered in glue and sequins brought a genuine smile to her face.

As she was fifteen minutes early, she pushed open the door without knocking, expecting the room to be empty. It wasn't. Harrison Mackenzie was already there, staring forlornly at the selection of teas on the sideboard, nary a Bedazzler or hot glue gun in sight.

He turned toward the door as she entered and his blue eyes widened momentarily. But that was the only sign that he recognized her from last night. Damn, he had control. What would it take to make him lose it? Why did she want to know?

"Perhaps I should introduce myself this time," she said, striding toward the tall man. His suit jacket lay across the back of one of the chairs, and she could testify that it wasn't padding making him look so built. The man was all muscle. "I'm Jade Irvine, your translator for the next few days."

"Harrison Mackenzie. But you already knew that, didn't you? I apologize for jumping to conclusions last night." His deep voice, his Canadian accent, the hint of remorse in his smile, and the way his gaze wouldn't drop below her lips sent a bolt of satisfaction through her. She'd confused him, and she liked that.

"You can make it up to me later," she replied with a wink. He'd seen her as a desirable woman. Now she had to impress him with her mind, or more specifically her tongue. Jesus, the things she'd like to do to him with her tongue. *Stop right there, Jade. He's your boss. Having fun is all well and good, but not if the result is career suicide.* "Are you looking for coffee?"

"I can make do with tea." He leaned against the table and raked her with his eyes. This time, they dipped below her lips and her body flooded with heat. "You speak Indonesian?"

"Yes. As well as Malay, Dutch, and Balinese. I've studied Javanese, but I'm not fluent. My mother was Indonesian, and I spent my early years in Bali." It was a part of her history that she'd recited a million times, so she could do it without the heart-wrenching pain that came with reliving the period following her mother's death.

Her idyllic childhood had morphed into a complete upheaval of her life—moving to Australia where her father was from, adjusting to a different culture, being shoved into a boarding school where she knew no one. Sucking in a deep breath, she pushed down the lump in her throat and concentrated on the task at hand.

She moved over to the hotel phone and dialed catering, ordering in Indonesian to prove she could speak the language.

"The coffee will be here in a minute. I am curious, however, why you need my services. I researched the companies you're dealing with, and all the senior staff speak English."

"Yes, but when they're not speaking English, I want to know what they're saying. I don't like being in the dark." For a second, his gaze swept the length of her before snapping back to her face. "Actually, you being part Australian will help. I'll introduce you as my colleague and perhaps you can discreetly translate when they're not speaking English."

She nodded. She'd done that before: translated what people said when they didn't think the other party could understand. But it meant getting up close and personal, often whispering in the client's ear to disguise the fact she understood. It was going to take every ounce of concentration she possessed to work that way with Mr. Ice-Hot.

How did his usual female colleagues handle him? Perhaps she could call his office and get some advice. *Hello, I'm working with Harrison for the next few days and was wondering how you stop yourself from jumping his bones. You don't, you say? You have sex in the office every day? Good to know.* The giggle that rose in her throat froze there when his glacier blue eyes met hers. Never mind. She'd probably get frostbite if she so much as undid one button on his crisp, white shirt.

The coffee arrived, and Jade almost sighed in relief. Finally, she had something to do with her hands that didn't involve slipping small plastic disks through tiny buttonholes. After pouring them both a cup, she stood awkwardly beside him as he sipped from the gold-rimmed mug.

She should sit to hide her shaking legs. But then he'd loom over her. Not that it made a huge difference—with her standing in heels, he still towered above her. She'd worked with a lot of powerful men, most of them over fifty, and she'd managed quite nicely. But this man was in a league of his own. Harrison seemed to suck all the oxygen from the room, leaving her breathless.

"May I ask what the meetings are in regard to? I was told you were in discussions with a specialized paint supply company and also garment manufacturers. Are you working on two different investments?"

He put down his cup, flipped open his briefcase, and withdrew several photos. "One project. I invested in a couple of science geeks who have developed a paint that, when applied to fabric, produces different designs under different light conditions. So a perfectly acceptable T-shirt suddenly becomes outrageous in a club under the black lights."

Interesting. Did the man beside her have a wild side? That would definitely be worth exploring. "What's the problem, then?"

"The paint isn't adhering correctly to the shirts."

"Why are you here and not the science geeks? Surely they'd be more qualified to find the solution."

He took another sip of his coffee and his gaze shifted over her shoulder. "They couldn't afford to travel."

"And it's your money invested, so you're the one with the skin in the game."

"It's more than that. I—"

Two men knocked on the open door before stepping across the threshold. "*Selamat pagi*," one of the men said. They were both in their late forties, possibly older, and dressed in suits, but they seemed ill at ease.

Jade just stopped herself from returning the greeting in Indonesian, remembering that she wasn't supposed to reveal that she spoke the language. "Good morning," she replied.

Harrison stepped around the table, and names were exchanged. He introduced her as a colleague but left her title blank. While she prepared tea for the newcomers, Harrison engaged in small talk with the men. She could sense his restlessness, but still, he adhered to the local custom of easing his way into a business discussion.

She took her seat next to him and pulled a pad of paper and pen from her bag, ready to make notes or write down anything the other men said in Indonesian. She expected to be a bit bored and schooled herself to remain attentive or at least look like she was listening. Soon, however, she was caught up in negotiations about problem solving and timelines for delivery. Harrison was firm but not belligerent, listening to the others but pressing for specific responses when required.

After almost an hour of discussion, Harrison

excused himself to get another cup of coffee from the urn, blaming jet lag for his tiredness. As he stepped away from the table, the two men across from where he'd been sitting began to speak among themselves. While not pretending to listen, Jade wrote down their conversation on her pad. She hid a smile—they were talking about her and how distracting she would be if they had to work with her every day. Odd how she'd thought the same about Harrison.

"We did not know you were bringing a colleague with you," one of the men commented as Harrison returned.

"It was a last-minute decision. Ms. Irvine is new to my company, and I wanted to oversee her training myself."

She passed him the pad of paper and his gaze swept over her after reading her notes. His lips tightened and when he handed the paper back to her, anger blazed in his eyes. Did he think she'd made it up to try and get his attention?

"Will you be accompanying us to the factory, Ms. Irvine? Or enjoying some of Bali's beautiful sights?" Mr. Ramprakesh, the more senior of the two gentlemen, asked. "My wife would be pleased to show you around."

"I'll come to the factory," she replied. "I'm looking forward to seeing your operation." Her words signaled the end of the discussion, and they moved on to the plant tour.

As she sat in the back seat of the small car a few minutes later, her thigh inches from Harrison's, she wasn't so sure this was still a good idea. Her attraction to Keith, even at the pinnacle of their relationship, had nothing on what she was beginning to feel for the man next to her.

What did they say about climbing out of the frying pan only to end up in the fire?

Chapter Three

Harrison glanced at the pad of paper Jade was holding. She was translating the conversation taking place in Indonesian in the front of the vehicle. Most of the discussion was about her and her body. The coffee he'd drunk roiled in his stomach. He knew women had a hard time in the workplace, but he'd never been a witness to such blatant sexual harassment before. And he'd put her in that position by asking her not to reveal she spoke their language.

Being half-Highlander, half-Asian, honor was hardwired into his DNA. It was just wrong to sit here, knowing they were being rude to her, and do nothing about it.

Am I any better? His chest tightened as his accusations from the night before played back in his mind. In his defense, Jade had been scantily dressed and had approached him after two other women had already offered him their services for the night. But he shouldn't have jumped to conclusions.

It was a damn good thing she couldn't read his mind. After she'd walked into the meeting room this morning, he'd nearly tossed his breakfast. He had to work with her for the next few days, possibly a week, depending on how the meetings went. And he was supposed to ignore the way she made his body ache with need? This was going to be the greatest test of his control yet.

Worse, not only was he physically attracted to her, but he enjoyed her company as well. She had a vivacity, a joie de vivre, that was sorely lacking in his life. She was the light to his darkness.

When we're done meeting with them, I want you to tell them off in Indonesian. He typed the words out on his phone and showed it to her.

A brilliant smile curved her lips and when she turned to him, her eyes danced with laughter. It was the same look they'd had this morning when she'd entered the room and found him waiting. He suppressed the answering upward tug of his own lips. He'd have to make it up to her for last night. Perhaps they could have dinner together and start again. *Yeah, that'll be great for my self-control.* Better to keep playing the bastard and maintain his iceman persona. He couldn't risk letting his emotions out.

Today, of all days, he needed to keep busy, keep distant, and keep from remembering. This should have been a date to celebrate for the rest of his life—his son's birthday. He rubbed the inside of his right forearm. Like an amputee who still feels the agony of a lost limb, the echo of the tattoo's pain was as sharp as when he'd had the date etched into his skin almost thirteen years before.

Finally, they pulled up in front of a large warehouse. The parking area was overgrown, and it appeared that any minute now, the encroaching jungle would take over. They were one step closer to hell, because it was even hotter and more humid than it had been on the coast. A trickle of sweat ran down Harrison's back. It became a torrent when Jade swiveled to get out of the vehicle and the hem of her dress slid up. She quickly corrected her wardrobe malfunction but not before he'd gotten a glimpse of a tattoo on her thigh. Did her ink symbolize a hidden pain? Or was it just decoration?

As she waited for him to join her, he noticed again the way she held her left hand, thumb and middle finger pressed together. He searched her eyes when they met his. Was her overt confidence simply a mask? He shoved his hand in his pocket to stop from lacing his fingers with hers. The desire to protect battled with his need to keep distance between them.

Inside the warehouse, the air was blissfully cool and they were led to an impeccable-looking room filled with chemical processing equipment. Mr. Ramprakesh introduced them to his lead chemist, whose English was limited.

With Mr. Ramprakesh acting as translator, the chemist ran them through the steps they'd taken to replicate the paint formula Steven and Mark had sent from Canada. The two teens had personally shown Harrison how they'd come up with the specialized paint and mixed a batch in front of him, so he could confirm the two processes were identical. Jade nodded along as the manager spoke, letting Harrison know that the translation was accurate.

"So you can see, Mr. Mackenzie, the problem is not at our end," Mr. Ramprakesh said at the end of the demonstration.

Damn. He'd been sure the issue was in the paint production. He'd hoped to have this solved so he could be on his way home sooner rather than later. His father had suffered a stroke recently and was undergoing a barrage of tests. Harrison needed to be there to support his parents.

"Have you tried your paint on a T-shirt to prove it works?" Jade asked. As she hadn't contributed much to the discussions, she probably wanted to cement the idea that she was indeed his colleague and not just a bit of fluff he'd brought along for some out-of-the-office action.

"Of course. But you are welcome to test it yourself," the less-senior of the two managers said.

They found a white piece of cloth and offered it to Jade. She glanced at Harrison, a question in her eyes, and he nodded. While she wrote something on the cloth with a small paint brush, the two managers showed Harrison the rest of their operation through the windows that looked out onto the production floor. Barrels of chemicals were lined against a wall. A forklift moved one into position, where two men wrestled the contents into a large steel vat.

Jade put the paintbrush down, and the chemist who had been watching her smiled. All Harrison could see were a few squiggles, and the two executives paid no attention to what she'd put on the fabric.

"Would you like to see the rest of the operation while we wait for the paint to dry?" the younger of the two men asked. He held out his arm, gesturing for Jade to go first. As the man was about to move behind her, Harrison stepped forward. After their lecherous comments in the car, there was no way he was letting either of them within an arm's length of her. He'd never forgive himself if harm came to her while she was in his employ.

The plant tour took almost forty-five minutes, and even Harrison was bored by the end of it. The managers seemed proud of what they'd built up, and rightly so. He knew from his research that they'd started the company five years ago and their main product was reflective paint for marine applications, which seemed odd, given their distance from the sea. But the location of the plant probably accounted for its affordability.

"You have no women on your workforce?" Jade asked as they were escorted back to the chemist's room.

"Out here in the countryside, the women stay at home and care for their families," Mr. Ramprakesh replied.

"And because you're misogynistic bastards," Jade said, so low only Harrison could hear.

The white cloth was laid out on a bench, the paint now invisible. A black light sat next to it, ready to be plugged in. They all gathered around, and when the message Jade had written was revealed, the two business owners were decidedly silent.

"It says, 'I understood everything you said' in Indonesian and Balinese," Jade whispered into his ear. The warmth of her breath slid under his collar, and a bolt of lust cleaved his good intentions in two.

He glared at the two chemical company owners. The color had drained from Mr. Ramprakesh's face, and the other man kept staring at the cloth, no doubt replaying in his mind all the disgusting things he'd said earlier.

Mr. Ramprakesh began to stammer out an apology but Jade cut him off, speaking rapidly in what Harrison assumed was Balinese, since it sounded slightly different from the Indonesian she'd spoken earlier when she'd ordered the coffee.

The two men hurried from the room, their apologies in English floating behind them. The chemist said something to Jade, then departed as well.

"I asked them to give us a few minutes," Jade said when the men had left.

"What did the chemist say?"

"That they're pigs, but honest ones. They've been working on the formula for weeks, trying to find cheaper materials that will do the same job and also make it dry faster, to speed up production."

"I'll take that into account when I speak to my partners about extending the contract once the initial term is over. Their attitude toward you will go in the negative column."

She crossed her arms over her chest. "That's fancy talk for a man who less than twenty-four hours ago accused me of being a prostitute."

"I apologize. Before you approached me, I'd already had two women offer me their services for the night. I jumped to conclusions. But I promise to make it up to you later." He could pretend that spending the evening with her was to atone for his error. But he knew, and she probably did too, that he would have asked her to dinner even if he didn't need to make it up to her. He'd never felt such an intense attraction to a woman before. And although absolutely nothing could come of it, it was a welcome distraction today. If there was one thing Jade could do, it was take his mind off his misery.

"Oh, trust me, you will." The wicked smile that accompanied her words sent a surge of heat to his groin. Before he could ask her what she meant, she continued, "But back to business. Any instructions for what else you want to accomplish here?"

"No, I think we're done. The paint works. It must be something in the way they're applying it to the T-shirts that's the problem."

"And when are you meeting with those people?"

"Tomorrow."

"Let's head back to the hotel, then." He nodded and followed her from the room. At the top of the stairs, she gestured for him to go first. "In case I fall, I'll have something soft to land on," she said with a laugh.

Her perfume, although subtle, surrounded him as they descended. He was the one in danger of falling. How could a woman he'd only just met unsettle him so much?

"Harrison…"

He turned once he'd reached the bottom. She was still two steps above him and her breasts were directly in his line of sight. Raising his eyes to hers was one of the hardest things he'd done in a long time.

"Yes, Jade?" He put as much "pissed-off lawyer" as he could into his tone, hoping to dissuade her flirtation, but all she did was laugh.

"I know exactly how you can make it up to me tonight."

It didn't matter what language she used—he was in deep shit.

Chapter Four

The drive back to Djimbaran was accomplished in relative silence. When they finally arrived at the hotel, Harrison thanked the men for showing him their factory and finished with an ominous sounding, "I'll be in touch."

After a weekend of heavy partying, a smart girl would order room service, watch a little TV, and go to bed, ready for tomorrow's round of "who said what." But since Keith's betrayal, Jade had decided that sensible was for other women. She was here to have fun. Wallowing in self-pity had never been her style. She wanted to seize the day and shake it for all it was worth.

And since Karly, Jules, and Lauren had already flown back to Australia, that only left Harrison for Jade to hang with. Glancing through her lashes at his stern face and starched demeanor, she wasn't sure if he was up to fun, but hey, she'd never been one to choose the easy course in life.

It could have been her training as a translator, or having had her world shattered at the age of ten, but whatever the cause, she'd learned to read people. Well, most people. She'd been completely wrong about her ex-boyfriend. Then again, he'd been deliberately devious.

Harrison's firmly entrenched mask appeared to be motivated more by self-defense than deceit. Twice today, she'd noticed him rubbing his inner arm as though easing an ache centered there. He was wounded, and she wouldn't leave him to face his demons alone. She just hoped it wouldn't backfire, like her attempted rescue of the koi fish at boarding school or the dozen other misadventures that had peppered her life.

"I'll meet you back here in an hour," she said. Her heels clicked across the marble lobby like a timer on a gameshow as they walked past the entrance to the hotel bar.

"Is there any point reminding you that I'm currently your boss?" Harrison raised one imperious eyebrow, which only made him look sexier.

"You're my boss while the meetings are in progress. Off the clock, you're just a guy who owes me a favor."

He cocked his head. "You're very sure of yourself."

"If I'm not, who will be?"

He glanced down at her hand and back at her face. "Can't argue with that." Although it looked like he wanted to. Instead he said, "All right. I'll meet you back here in an hour."

"Wear something casual."

"I don't do casual." He spun on his heel and headed toward the lifts.

He was in the lobby waiting when she returned fifty-eight minutes later. His concession to casual had been to remove his tie and undo one button on his shirt. And still he managed to look hotter than any other man she'd seen in recent history. If he dropped his jacket, revealing all those mouth-watering muscles, she'd probably be trampled by other women rushing to be near him.

"Okay, I'm here. Where are you taking me?" He shoved his hands in his trouser pockets, but based on the way his eyes blazed, that had more to do with keeping his hands off her than adopting an aggressive stance.

She'd tried for the sweet spot between her outfit from last night and the strictly business attire of today. Her flowy skirt came respectably to just above her knees, and her top, while off the shoulder, kept the girls covered in two layers of fabric. No nipple-gate tonight.

"I think it's rather a question of where you're taking me," she replied.

"You didn't tell me to make reservations. I hope you're happy with a street food stall for dinner."

"Hey, I spend almost as much time in Bali as in Australia these days. My digestive tract has adjusted. Can you say the same? Or should I teach you how to say, 'Where's the loo?' in Indonesian?"

"Point taken. However, I believe it's the custom for you, as a local, to be hospitable and show me the best place to eat."

"Challenge accepted." She resisted the urge to slip her arm through his as they stepped out of the air-conditioned hotel into the warm evening air. If they hurried, they could still catch the sunset from Rock Bar.

After arguing with the taxi driver about the fare, Jade sat back and let the chaos that was Indonesia surround her. Scooters loaded with goods or people, sometimes both, wove between cars and pedestrians. Stray dogs and the occasional chicken roamed unchecked. It was life at its least pretentious. And she loved it.

"Where are we going?" Harrison asked as the traffic thinned and they drove along the coast. He'd taken off his jacket and now rolled the sleeves back on his shirt, revealing muscled forearms and, shockingly, a small tattoo on the spot he'd been rubbing throughout the day. It looked like a name and date, but without grabbing his arm and holding it up, she couldn't read it. She'd never have pegged him for an inked man.

Whoa, did Harrison have an inner bad boy? Her mouth watered. *Careful, girl.* There was seizing the day—or in this case, the man—and there was getting fired and damaging her reputation. Maybe for once in her life, she should look before she leaped. *But where's the fun in that?*

"We're headed to a little bar known for its spectacular sunsets. Then there's a great seafood restaurant down on the beach and a hot club we can hit afterward."

"Yes to the bar and restaurant. No to the club."

"We'll see," she replied. She'd probably be too tired to hit the dance floor, but she wasn't about to let him off the hook that easy.

Her Balinese and whatever Harrison slipped to the maître d' got them a prime spot on the balcony, overlooking the sea. A warm breeze ruffled her skirt and blew a strand of hair into her eyes. Before she could move it, Harrison reached across and tucked it behind her ear, his fingers lingering for a moment on the strand. The intimacy of the touch knocked her cockiness down a notch. God, how she wanted to lean into his touch, rub her cheek on the back of his hand before dropping a kiss there.

Maybe Karly is right. Maybe I'm the one who could do with some fixing. 'Cause there is no way I should be this attracted to a closed-off Canadian venture capitalist who is also currently my boss—no matter how high he ranks on Lauren's hotness scale.

What the hell was it with this guy? She usually had way more self-control. She could only claim fatigue and the fact that her best friend was getting married, while Jade's love life was as barren as the Australian outback. Not that she was looking for love. But a semi-casual relationship would be good about now. Someone she could take to Karly's wedding and go to the pictures with from time to time.

The waiter took their drinks order, and Jade observed Harrison out of the corner of her eye as they watched the sun sink below the horizon. The sky was tinged with pinks, purples, and oranges, rivaling any decorator's color swatches.

"It's amazing," Harrison said, his voice reverential.

"Everyone has to see the sunset at least once when they visit Bali." She forced her eyes back to the rapidly darkening skyline and away from the interesting face of her companion. She could spend hours staring at him and still find something new to fascinate her. Like the tiny scar just above his left eyebrow, barely discernable yet shrieking that it had a story to tell.

The waiter brought their drinks and she took a long sip of her cocktail, trying to come up with a non-inflammatory topic of conversation. Harrison's index finger circled the rim of his neat whisky.

"Is this your first trip to Indonesia?"

His gaze swung back to her, and in the flickering candlelight, she saw a hint of sadness in his eyes. It was soon replaced with the aloofness he wore like protective armor. Her empathetic instincts set off an alarm. Forget her dead love life and her inconvenient attraction to him. This man had bigger problems needing attention.

"Yes. Although I've visited Singapore and Malaysia and recently Thailand when my business partner got married. And, of course, Korea, where my grandparents live."

"Ah, I was wondering about your heritage. Where did you get your blue eyes?"

"My father. He's originally from Scotland."

Harrison was half-Scottish. Could he get any hotter? Outlander's Jamie Fraser had just slipped a spot in her "Scots I'd do in a heartbeat" list. "Do you have a kilt?"

A smile tugged the corner of his lips upward. "Not

with me."

Probably a good thing. Her self-control definitely wasn't ready for Harrison Mackenzie in a kilt. "Will you be staying after your business is concluded or heading straight back to Canada?" Her mind whirled with activities they could enjoy, should he have some free time, most of them involving Harrison in a swimsuit. *Geez, Jade, find a new record to play.*

"I have a flight booked for Saturday. I hope to be done by then."

"Well, if you finish before the weekend, I can give you some pointers on the best places to surf or eat or visit. What kind of thing interests you?"

"I'm not here on holiday. When my meetings wrap up, I'll leave."

"Shame. Bali has a lot to offer. Even for someone like you." *Oh God, where has my brain-mouth filter gone now?*

He put down his whisky and crossed his arms over his chest. "Someone like me?"

"Someone in need of a good vacation. When's the last time you relaxed?"

"I'm relaxed now."

"Really? You've got your arms crossed, your shirt buttoned up to your neck, and I swear I can see you mentally responding to emails."

His eyes flashed with a hint of annoyance. "What's it to you?"

"I've worked with a lot of different people who come to Indonesia to do business. And basically, they fall into two types. There are ones who take the time to absorb the culture and enjoy the experience. They ask me to take them to little shops off the tourist routes so they can buy genuine souvenirs to take back home to loved ones. They try new things and leave here a happier person."

"And the second type?"

"They come here for the same reason, but they're determined to keep it all business. When their meetings are done for the day, they order room service and watch CNN or BBC News. They pick up presents for their kids at the airport and never feel the sand between their toes."

"I'm here to do business. Whether I get sand in my socks or buy my knickknacks from the airport, it makes no difference in the end."

She drained her drink and sat back in her chair. "That's where you're wrong."

"Excuse me?"

"Bali is special. If you let it, it can heal your soul."

"My soul is just fine. I didn't come here for some *Eat Pray Love* transformation."

"Shame. I make a mean mixed tape."

He burst out laughing, and Jade sucked in a breath. Talk about transformations.

Her voice was a little shaky when she asked, "Are you actually telling me you've read the book?"

"Watched the movie with my mother one Christmas. I hated it."

Still, he must have sat through to the end to know the thing about the mixed tapes. A guy who would watch a chick flick with no hope of getting laid had to have some heart. Even if it was all for his mother.

What kind of woman would it take to make him shed his restraint and enjoy life? Why did she even care? She wasn't looking to get involved with anyone, especially not with someone as closed off as Harrison. But dammit, he did intrigue her. And he needed her help.

Based on past experience, that was usually where things went horribly wrong.

Chapter Five

She had to give it to him. Even stiff as a board, he was an entertaining dinner date, telling her about some of the crazy inventions that had been pitched to him and his friend and business partner Caleb. Like, really? People thought toeless socks—"so you could keep your feet warm but still show off your pedicure"— were a good idea? Wasn't that why impractical, but at least partially fashionable, peep-toe boots were popular?

Apart from working together, the two lifelong friends also had some sort of good-natured war going about which country made the best whisky. She had to remember to order scotch when she was with Harrison or risk a frown of disapproval. *Not that I want his approval or anything.* Oh God, her plan to help him was already on the rocks. *Kind of like his whisky. Dammit, no one needs an inner punster, Jade.* She battled a stupid smile and lost.

At least she wasn't the only one who wanted to impress. He had the wait staff rushing to do his bidding with just a flick of his hand. And it wasn't about the sizable tip they expected either. He gave off a vibe that made people want to please him.

"Tell me about life in Canada," she said as the waiter cleared their plates and she sat back to finish the last of her wine. Between the sunset cocktail and most of a bottle of wine, she had a pretty good buzz going. "I've always wanted to go there."

"I live on the west coast, so the climate is a lot milder than the rest of the country. We have mountains and the ocean, so technically you could swim in the morning and ski in the afternoon. But the water is pretty cold, no matter what time of year it is, so I don't recommend it."

"Sounds beautiful."

"It is."

"And you've always lived there?"

"Yes. What about you—were you born here in Bali?" he asked.

"Yes. My parents owned a resort just down the coast. Nothing as grand as the place we're staying, but nice enough. My dad came over on holiday, met my mum, and fell in love with both her and the island."

He glanced around, and then his gaze locked with hers for a long moment. "I can understand that." He grabbed for his glass of water as though he'd been trekking in the desert for six hours without a drop to drink. After draining half of it, he asked, "When did you move to Australia?"

She took a sip of wine to cover her reaction to the admiration she'd seen in his eyes. "When I was eleven. About a year after my mum died." Raising her eyes, she glanced at her companion. Maybe that was why she was so drawn to Harrison. He had the same melancholy around him that her dad had had during those dark days.

Harrison's cool detachment warmed briefly. "Sorry to hear about your mother."

"Thanks. My memories are faded now, but I remember she had a beautiful smile."

"You seem to have inherited that from her." The compliment fell from his lips with such practiced ease that she wondered if it was genuine. Then for the first time, his eyes lit with laughter, transforming his whole demeanor. And her heart rate went into triple digits. "My mother drives me crazy more often than not. But I can't imagine life without her. It must have been hard: losing a parent and relocating to a new country."

"Yes. I was given a choice. My Indonesian family wanted me to stay with them when my father decided to move back to Australia. He said he couldn't bear to remain where everything reminded him of the woman he'd loved and lost. But I didn't want to leave my dad alone, so I went as well."

Harrison's hand inched toward hers on the table, retreating before he made contact. "But things worked out once you were in Australia?"

"Eventually." She hadn't even been in Oz two weeks before her dad had shipped her off to boarding school. Bali hadn't been the only thing that reminded him of her mother. Those first months in a new environment had been tough. For her father's sake, she'd put on a false smile and brightness whenever he'd visited or called, not wanting to add to his burden. And to cope with the bullies who'd targeted an awkward girl with a funny accent, she'd adopted an air of supreme confidence, as if nothing could touch her.

Eventually, she'd met Karly, Jules, and Lauren, so it had all turned out okay in the end. Those three became the family she'd needed until her father had recovered enough to spend time with her again.

As if sensing the conversation had drifted into choppy emotional waters, Harrison made a strategic change of subject. "How long have you been translating?"

"More than five years now. I get about seventy-five percent of my assignments in Australia, mostly illegal immigrant cases. I do some written work, but I prefer live translation. When an opportunity comes up to work in Bali or one of the other islands, I jump at it."

Once again, his gaze lingered on her face. "I'm glad you took this assignment."

Was he really happy they'd met? But even she didn't have enough bravado to ask. Instead, she said, "What's the plan for tomorrow? Do you want me to pretend to be your colleague again and translate surreptitiously?"

"No, I'm not up for another day of knowing other men are discussing your body."

She tried a laugh, but it was strained. "That was rather epic."

"The word you're looking for is *disgusting*." He had that distant look in his eyes again.

They could both do with a diversion. "Hey, if you don't want to go clubbing, what do you say we drive to the paint factory, break in, and leave some cut durian around their offices?"

"Durian?"

"It's a fruit that is renowned for its stink. Richard Sterling, a travel writer, said it smelled like 'pig shit, onions, and turpentine garnished with a gym sock.'"

"Sounds dreadful. Why is it even grown?"

"The taste is amazing, once you get past the aroma. It's also the perfect revenge fruit. It will take them hours, if not days, to get rid of the smell."

He looked at her for a moment as if she'd lost her mind then burst out laughing. "I don't know whether to applaud your inventiveness or be afraid that you're serious."

"You didn't speak with any of my friends while they were here, did you?"

"No. Why?"

"No reason." She heaved a fake sigh to pretend she'd only been joking about the durian. "Since the factory is on the other side of the island, and we do have to work in the morning, maybe we'd better stick a pin in that idea."

He opened his mouth, closed it, then tried again. "Let's play it straight tomorrow. You're my translator, there to help if things get confusing."

"Excellent. And we're meeting with the people who put the paint on the shirts? Where do the shirts come from?"

"Yes, tomorrow's meeting is with the silk screeners. The shirts are sourced from another supplier, and we'll meet with them on Thursday if needed. The problem must be with the paint application process."

She shrugged. Perversely, she hoped it wasn't, so that the assignment would last as long as possible. Harrison was an enigma, and she was intrigued—even if, at the moment, he seemed more like the bedazzling sort than a break-and-enter accomplice. Still, given enough time, she could probably fix that too.

They both declined dessert and Harrison paid the bill, although she offered to split it with him. As she stood, the world shifted beneath her. His arm went around her waist to keep her upright but stayed there after she regained her balance. It was worth faking a sudden attack of vertigo to stay in his arms a little longer. His hand on her waist was firm, his strength undeniable. The heat from his body was more intoxicating than alcohol.

"I want to walk on the beach before we go back," she said.

"Do you think that's wise? You seem a bit … wobbly."

"Screw wise. It's just the wine. Besides, you're not going home without at least a little sand in your socks." She leaned further into him and slipped her shoes off. Suddenly ten centimeters shorter, he towered over her.

"I'm not taking my shoes off," he said, looking at her with exasperation.

"Then they're going to get very wet." She grabbed his hand and ran for the water's edge. He let her drag him behind her because there was no way she could have moved him if he hadn't wanted to come.

"All right." He stopped a meter from the water,

released her hand, and bent down to slip off his shoes and socks and roll his trousers to mid-calf. When he was finally barefoot, he gazed up at her. "Happy?"

"Oh, petal, you'll have to take off more than your footwear to make me happy."

He raised his imperious eyebrows at her again. "You're incorrigible. Are you like this with all your translation assignments?"

"Nope. You get special treatment because I like you." Okay, that was definitely the wine talking. Before she could blurt out anything else stupid, she grabbed his hand again and led him to the water. As the cool, wet sand squidged between her toes, she released a sigh. It didn't matter how many times she did this, it always felt amazing. "I don't think I could live anywhere without a beach."

"I feel the same about the mountains. Even though I rarely get to spend much time in them, just knowing they're there, waiting, ready to embrace me in their magnificence…"

Ah, so the man did have a poetic soul. It was just buried under too much venture capitalist crap.

They walked along the water's edge, the occasional wave splashing up on her calves, but the reef took most of the ocean's force and tamed it.

"Do you enjoy what you do?" she asked as the silence lengthened. This part of the beach was lined with restaurants and night clubs, so there was enough light spilling onto the sand that they could see where they were going.

"I enjoy helping people with a passion for what

they've invented. Some of the products are practical, some are quirky, and some are just for entertainment purposes. But by helping people with a financial leg up, in a way I can change their lives."

"So it's not just about the money for you?"

"No. I was lucky in my first investment. I backed one of those online games that went viral."

She thought for a moment about which games had been popular recently. "Oh. My. God. Are you responsible for Ninja Nanas?"

"Guilty."

"Do you know how many hours I wasted playing that?"

"No idea. I never got beyond level one."

Another couple walking ahead of them turned at the sound of her laughter. "You're still a Knitting Nana?" she asked when she had the breath to talk again.

Harrison straightened his shoulders. "We can't all be Assasi-Nanas. Besides…" He unleashed a killer smile that turned her legs to butterscotch pudding. "I have other ways of bringing my enemies to their knees."

I am doomed.

"What is it about the T-shirts that made you want to invest in them? You don't seem the kind of guy to worry about having something cool to wear when you go clubbing." Although she still wasn't ready to give up the vision of him with a glue gun.

"I couldn't care less about the product. I invested in the two teenagers who came up with the idea. They both come from lower-income backgrounds, and getting this to market would not only allow them to go to university but would help their families as well."

She stopped walking so she could look at his face. That hint of sadness was back in his eyes. Then he blinked, and it disappeared.

"What were you like as a teenager? I bet you were a straight-A student and on the debate team."

"Actually, I was a jock. I had to be tutored"— there was a catch in his voice at odds with the conversation—"just to get passing grades." He dropped his shoes and tugged them on, wet sand and all, shoving his socks in his pockets. "You done here?" Without waiting for her reply, he headed to the top of the beach.

His abrupt transition back to impenetrable businessman nearly knocked her over like a rogue wave. She raced after him. It seemed it was her turn to apologize.

But for what?

Chapter Six

Jade finally caught up with him at the edge of the sand. "Harrison, I'm sorry." Her breathless voice sent heat flooding through him.

He'd been rude to walk away from her, but it was either that or scream in agony. It was bad enough being reminded about how stupid he'd been as a teenager. Today, on what would have been his son's thirteenth birthday, the pain was almost unbearable. One of the reasons he'd taken this trip to Indonesia had been to escape his well-meaning family and their annual tribute to the infant who'd never even had a chance at life. And dinner with Jade was supposed to take his mind off his past, not serve it up on a sandy platter.

Had Bryce lived, he would be a teenager now. Would he have been an athlete like his father? Or a brainiac like his mother?

Harrison had to clear his throat before he could reply. "It's late. I want to go back to the hotel." He flagged down a taxi and waited while Jade slipped her shoes back on. She held onto him as she adjusted the straps of her sandals, her hand resting on his arm where he'd had his son's name and date of birth tattooed into his skin—the eternal reminder of what happened when he lost control.

"I didn't mean to upset you," she said as they slid into the backseat of the taxi.

He gave the driver the name of their hotel, not caring if they took the long way back and it cost more. It would delay the moment when he stood in the well-lit lobby and had to face the questions in Jade's eyes. He just knew she wasn't going to let this go.

"I realized how late it was and I still have to prepare for tomorrow's meeting."

"You're a terrible liar." Jade crossed her arms over her stomach which pushed up her full breasts. He forced his eyes to the windshield, but there wasn't much to see there except the back of an overloaded minivan spewing diesel fumes into the air.

"For someone who specializes in understanding people, you should know when a conversation is over."

"Ah, but that's the problem. I want to understand people, and your one-eighty shift when I mentioned your teenage years has me puzzled." She tilted her head, and when he attempted to turn away again, she put her hand on his cheek and drew his face back to hers. "You're in pain, and I don't know what I said or did to cause it."

"You did nothing. Can you please drop the subject?"

Any polite person in the entire world would have agreed to his request. He had to be stuck in traffic, in a taxi with no air conditioning and the one person who didn't know when to leave things be. "Bali can't fix you unless it knows what the problem is."

"I told you, I don't need fixing."

"There you go, lying again—"

"Bali can't bring back my dead son. Or my wife, who I ruined with my loss of control. Bali can't make me forget the two lives I destroyed. Or dull the pain that gnaws at me every morning when I get up and remember that because of my stupidity, they will never see an amazing sunset like I did tonight. Bali is not strong enough, despite what you or *Eat Pray Love* may say." He ran a hand through his hair, tugging on the strands to deflect the agony. He hated himself for his loss of control. Then and now.

Anyone else would have mumbled something incoherent and then stared out their window in silence for the rest of the journey. But he was with Jade. She pivoted on the seat, grabbed his head with both hands, and pulled it down toward hers. Her lips met his in a kiss he guessed was meant to comfort, but it quickly transformed into an all-out assault on his senses.

For just one night, he wanted to feel something other than heartache. And Jade was the one woman able to do that for him. Her body responded to his, and she straddled him to get even closer. It was too much. Too out of control. Too … perfect.

His hands rested on her hips, ostensibly to move her off his lap. Instead they crept up her sides until they found her breasts. The rest of his body went on high alert. His tongue dueled with hers, savoring the taste of her, the hint of wine, the spice of the curry she'd eaten, the sheer mind-blowing pleasure of having a willing, beautiful woman in his arms.

He had to get a grip, now, before the taxi driver pulled over and threw them out of the cab in the middle of the street. He forced his hands back down to her hips and his tongue back into his own mouth.

"Jade." His voice sounded like he'd been gargling gravel.

She tucked her head in his neck. Her rapid breathing pushed her breasts against his chest while the warm air she expelled went straight down his shirt. When she eventually raised her head, her eyes were full of laughter. Did this woman have a serious bone in her body? "Should I apologize again?"

"I'd settle for you getting off my lap."

Jade swung her leg back over, the movement of her skirt revealing her tattoo. Was it as significant to her as his was to him?

"I don't know what overcame me," she said, smoothing her hair, which had been pulled out of its neat bun at the back of her head. Had he done that? He flexed his hand, and the memory of the silky strands sliding between his fingers came back to him.

"Can we blame it on Bali?" he asked, struggling to surface from the tide of desire washing through him.

"Or the cocktails and wine."

"Noted." He ran his hands down his pants, not because his palms were damp but to try and erase the feel of Jade on his thighs. He'd never met a woman as potent as her. A woman who wore sensuality like a perfume and grabbed life by the balls.

His wife Emily had been quiet and sweet. Her innocence, despite her turbulent home life, was one of the many things he'd loved about her. Her vulnerability and fragility had brought out the protector in him. Except he'd been the one to lead her to destruction.

It would probably take a hell of a lot to break Jade, although he'd had a glimpse of an artfully hidden tender heart when she let down her guard. Especially when she spoke of her mother's death. She was a woman who felt deeply. Which, given their mutual attraction, could be dangerous. He had no love left in him to give. If he bent even one silky strand of her ebony hair, he'd never forgive himself. Not that there was any self-forgiveness left in him either.

But worse than what he could do to her was what she could do to him.

She could make him forget.

***

As Jade hurried toward the conference room, yesterday's cocky smile was decidedly absent. She'd given up the high ground last night when she'd attacked Harrison in the taxi on the way back to the hotel.

He'd been kind enough to accept her excuse that she'd been drunk, even though they both knew that wasn't the case. She could pretend to herself that she'd been trying to make him feel better after his confession about his wife's and son's deaths. Whatever happened, he clearly blamed himself, although she found it incredibly difficult to believe Harrison was capable of harming anyone.

Deep down, though, she knew the truth. That kiss had been all for her. She'd waited for him to make the move, and when he hadn't, she'd attacked him. Threw herself at a man grieving the loss of his spouse and child. What was wrong with her?

The worst thing was that she didn't even regret it. Harrison had kissed her back in a few seconds of forgetfulness, and it had been fantastic. She'd always figured that kisses were kisses, some slightly better than others depending on technique and what the person had recently eaten. Her new boss had wiped that perception off the table.

As with yesterday, he was already in the conference room, cradling a cup of coffee. She'd made sure it was on order before she'd gone to bed. For just a moment, she stared, letting his gorgeousness brighten her day.

"Good morning," she said as she stepped into the room. "Glad the coffee arrived today." When he didn't reply right away, she finally forced her gaze to his, expecting censure or at least disapproval. Instead she found humor.

"How's your head this morning?" he asked.

Ah, they were still going with the drunk excuse. But she was honest to a fault, even with herself … unless it involved bubble tsunamis. "You know I wasn't drunk when I sexually assaulted you last night. I understand if you'd rather have someone else translate for you. I've already contacted my agency, and they can have another person here within an hour."

"I don't want another translator. I'm not sure your minor indiscretion last night compares with my huge gaffe, but I'm willing to call us even if you are. And for the record, I didn't consider that an assault on my person."

"Well, okay, thank you." At least he'd taken it in his stride. But it didn't negate the fact that they'd shared a moment. One she'd like to repeat, over and over again.

Fortunately, she was saved the embarrassment of a further rehash of events by the arrival of three men from the silk screener's. Harrison introduced her as his translator, and she could read the relief on the newcomers' faces when they realized they wouldn't need to converse in English.

These men were much more polite than the two from the day before—whether because they knew she could understand them or because they were nicer people, she wasn't sure. But after exchanging pleasantries for a while, the meeting got underway. Again, they claimed not to understand why the paint wasn't adhering to the shirts properly, saying they had followed the instructions as delivered and had an extensive history of customer satisfaction.

Harrison was pleasant and charming, but his mounting frustration was evident in the repeated clenching of his fist under the table and his fidgeting leg. He clearly wanted to get this sorted so he could leave Indonesia and get back to his life in Canada. However, it seemed another site visit was called for. But due to a scheduling problem, it would have to take place the next morning. Which left them with the rest of the day free.

As the three men departed, Harrison raked a hand through his hair. Jade was sure if she left him, he'd spend the day working in his hotel room. And that would be a tragedy on the beautiful island of Bali.

"We crossed off getting sand in your socks last night. Do you want to go snorkeling? The coral reefs off Bali are some of the world's best. Or would you prefer to do some sightseeing?"

He seemed confused by both her suggestions. "I want to go back to my room and prepare for the meetings I have next week."

"Aarrrnn." She made a noise like a wrong-answer buzzer on a game show. "I'm not going to let you spend a beautiful day working inside."

He crossed his arms and leaned against the table, but there was a hint of amusement around his lips. "You're not? Who made you master over my life? We're even now. You can't coerce me into coming with you because I owe you one."

"I don't coerce, I persuade." She twirled a strand of her hair around her finger. "I guess I'll just have to explore all by myself. I hope I don't get lost or anything bad happens to me. I'm sure you'll be able to work just fine not worrying about where I am or what I'm doing…"

He stopped leaning against the table and came to stand directly in front of her. She'd worn a pair of flat shoes today, so his height was emphasized. He took the strand of hair she'd been twirling and curled it around his index finger. "This is your homeland. I'm positive you'll be safe."

"What if I say I don't want to go alone?" She bit her bottom lip, waiting for his reply. She was playing with fire. And worse than the threat of being expelled from boarding school for setting the kitchen ablaze, getting involved with a man as badly damaged as Harrison could have lasting consequences. But when she gazed up into his blue eyes, she couldn't retract the offer. This man, even while hurting, drew her like a magnet. He was honorable, honest, and intensely loyal to friends and family.

She wanted to make him smile, see his eyes light with joy and laughter as they had last night at dinner. She wanted to know what made him tick, what could make him forget his past and look to the future. Yup, she was well and truly in over her head.

But when adventure called, Jade answered on the first ring.

He unwound her hair and tucked the strand behind her ear, his fingers grazing her neck as he did, and a shiver of awareness coursed through her.

"Then if you ask me nicely, I might reconsider."

She needed to rethink this. The scent of his cologne filled her head, and she had to stop herself from going up on tiptoe and licking him. Instead, she batted her eyelashes for good measure. "Harrison, will you come with me this afternoon?"

A wicked grin lifted his lips. "It would be my pleasure."

Oh. God. What have I done?

Chapter Seven

The woman was insane. Or maybe it was him. Why could he not resist her? Last night's kiss in the taxi had kept him awake for hours, reliving the feel and taste of her, longing for more. He'd had the perfect opportunity to take a step back and get some perspective, but no. Here he was, waiting in the hotel lobby to spend the day with her. Just the two of them. No business discussions or problems to solve to take his mind off her body and what his wanted to do with it.

It was utterly ridiculous. But he couldn't get enough of her smile, of seeing her emerald eyes light up when something amused her. Which happened a lot. She had a way of looking at the world that he envied, as if every obstacle was a potential adventure. He wanted to bask in her sunshine, let her light up every dark corner of his soul until there was no more pain inside him. *Impossible.* But irrationally, he itched to test his theory.

The elevator doors opened, and she strolled out wearing a pair of cut-off jean shorts and a red-and-white polka-dot halter top. Her shoulders were bare, and with so much golden skin on display, he quickly glanced down at his phone to hide the desire in his eyes. It would be easy to come up with some excuse, a phone call or message that required his urgent attention, to get out of spending the day with her.

But when her exotic perfume filled his nose … it was game over. For once, he was going to enjoy himself, spend time in the company of a beautiful woman, and forget the tragedy of his past and all the promises he'd made standing over his wife's grave. Today he was going to let Bali have its way with him.

"So, where do you want to go?" Jade tipped her face up, and he had to clench his hands into fists to stop from pulling her against him for a kiss. Her joie de vivre was contagious.

"I'm interested in ancient civilizations. Any ruins or old monuments we can go see?"

She tapped a now-crimson-colored nail on her lower lip before replying, "I know just the place to take you. Glad to see you got into the spirit of things and changed into shorts and a short-sleeved shirt." Her eyes raked over him, and he shifted his weight slightly so his hard-on wasn't quite as visible. From the awareness in her eyes as they met his, she'd noticed.

"How are we going to get there?" he asked as they stepped out of the hotel into the sweaty air. At least the presence of a taxi driver and other tourists at the destination would help keep a check on his lust.

"I'm driving. I hope your medical insurance is up to date." Her laugh tugged an answering smile from him.

Did Jade's laugh sound slightly maniacal?

She led him around the hotel and across the street to a battered Jeep that was old enough to have seen action in World War II.

"I can see why you wanted someone to come with you," he said. "This doesn't look like it'll make it to the end of the block without breaking down."

"Don't knock Sherman. He's got plenty of miles still left in him." Climbing behind the wheel, her shorts rode up to show her tattoo.

He reached out and traced the ink with his finger, smiling as a tremor swept through her. "What does this say?" He'd seen enough Balinese writing now to identify the script.

"If you can read this, you're too close," she replied, pulling down the hem of her shorts to cover the ink.

Yeah, right, and I'm Chris Hemsworth. But he didn't want to get into a discussion about tattoos, because he wasn't ready to share the meaning behind his. Today was supposed to be about fun.

As they left behind the town and its chaos, Jade pointed out her favorite beaches, cafés, places to buy souvenirs, the house of a friend or someone important. Even her first school. Then she turned inland, and the road got steep and narrow. He hung onto the door frame to stop himself from flying into Jade, even with his seatbelt on. Rather than slow down, she took the corners as if she were in a racing car, not a Jeep whose suspension predated the wheel.

"We're not going to see much if we die before we get there," he shouted over the flapping of the canvas behind him. A few of the snaps holding down the roof were no longer attached to the vehicle.

All Jade did was laugh—definitely maniacal.

When she pulled into a deserted parking lot—at least, that's what he assumed the flat piece of land was supposed to be—he had to stop himself from kissing the ground. Thrill rides had never been his thing.

"Where are we?" Perched on the side of the mountain as they were, the town where the hotel was located was just visible along with the miles of white-sand beach hugging the coastline. Here, the air was cooler, fresher, and he pulled in a deep, calming breath. It was spectacular. He'd have to thank Jade for showing this to him. But not just yet—he didn't want to transfer too much ammunition into her hands.

She pulled a pair of hiking boots out of the back of her Jeep and leaned a large stick against the side while she replaced her footwear. He turned back to the vista, since watching her put one foot up on the bumper to tie her laces, revealing even more of her long legs, was making him uncomfortably warm again.

"There's an old Buddhist monastery and a few other buildings just behind those boulders," she said, pointing behind her. "Archaeologists haven't finished excavating the site, so there are no plaques or anything to say what the various piles of stones are. But one of my cousins worked here for a summer when he was in university and he showed me around. I thought you might like it better than the other places that are crowded with tourists."

"Sounds interesting. Are you sure it's okay that we're here?" He did not need to be arrested for trespassing on an ancient religious site.

"I'm sure it's okay," she said with a shrug. "Are you coming, or do you want to stand here and watch for the archeological police?" She grabbed her stick and was about to hoist a backpack when he took it from her and put it on his own shoulder. Plastic water bottles knocked into each other within the pack as he followed her toward a gap in the boulders.

"I'm coming. But only to make sure you don't get in trouble."

She laughed. "Good luck with that. Many before you have tried and failed."

That, he didn't doubt. But the lure of an ancient site, free of other people, was like a bottle of pinot grigio to a bored suburban housewife.

As Jade walked, she banged her stick on the ground and used it to move some of the vegetation out of the way. "I'm not too fond of snakes," she said in response to his raised eyebrow.

"Want me to go in front?" Because walking behind her, staring at her firm ass in her tight shorts, was more dangerous to him than any reptile.

"You don't know where you're going," she replied.

Straight to hell if I keep imagining taking you from behind while you're bent over an ancient altar.

"Do you?" he asked.

Her laughter caused something in the undergrowth to scurry away, and his shorts to get too tight. Maybe he should start wearing a sarong.

"Not usually, but in this case, I do." She veered to

the left at a dead tree, and after another ten meters, they entered a large clearing. Although the vegetation had been cut back some time in the past, it hadn't lost its untainted feel. A few grid markers were still in situ from the archaeological dig, but other parts appeared unexplored. The place was amazing.

He headed over to a set of statues of women holding urns. Four hundred years ago, water would have spurted from them, allowing the monks to cleanse themselves before entering the temple. Behind the statues, roughhewn stones were tumbled on top of each other like an abandoned game of giant Jenga.

"They say the temple building was three stories tall and would have housed a hundred monks at its peak." Jade spoke softly as though in awe of the place as well.

"Thank you for bringing me here."

A devilish smile rivaled the wicked gleam in her eyes. "My pleasure."

Yup, he was going straight to hell.

***

The sun warmed her back as she sat on a fallen piece of the temple and watched Harrison wander around the site. He took hundreds of photos, although to her, one tumbled-down boulder looked just like the rest. Still, he was happy, and his whole body vibrated with excitement—over a bunch of broke-down buildings. He reminded her of Indiana Jones. Did he have a fedora and whip? This could get interesting.

Harrison was a paradox, a mystery she was enticed to solve. She already knew he loved his family and friends. He spoke intelligently on everything from sports to world politics—holding his own opinions but allowing others to express theirs.

In those odd moments when Harrison forgot his past, he was a different man—one who laughed heartily, kissed with passion, and made her insides melt with a look. That was the man she wanted to uncover, the one she was seeing more of the longer she spent in his company. She unscrewed the cap on a bottle of water and took a sip. Harrison was so engrossed in the ruins, would he even notice if she tipped the rest of the water down her chest?

As if sensing she was thinking of him, he turned and strode toward her, his eyes caressing her as he walked. And for once, he didn't try to disguise his interest. Now her front was even warmer than her back. If she doused herself, the water would probably sizzle off her.

"Got any more of that?" He sat on another fallen bit of masonry and stretched his long legs out in front of him.

Jade handed him the other bottle, deliberately brushing her hand against his thigh as she did so. "Why do you like history so much?"

He took a long drink. "No one has ever asked me that before."

"It's also not an answer."

He searched her face. "I guess it's because I believe if we learn from the past, we may not repeat as many mistakes." His eyes turned serious, and although he looked out over the temple ruins, she sensed he was really searching inward.

She reached over and placed her hand on his. "Sometimes, the lesson to learn is that there's nothing we can do except concentrate on the future. My dad eventually got over my mother's death, and now he's happily married again."

"I'm glad for him. And you." He pulled in a deep breath. "This site is amazing. Thanks for showing it to me."

And that was all the personal revelations she was going to get out of him. "If you're really interested, I can call my cousin and see if he can meet us here. He'll be able to tell you what used to go where."

Harrison was shaking his head before she even finished the sentence. "I like it being just the two of us. I can use my imagination."

His imagination could be put to way better use.

"Save some of that creativity. I haven't shown you the best part yet."

Water spurted from the bottle as he crushed it in his fist. "The best part?"

"Follow me." She put a bit more sway in her hips as she led the way across the site. It took three tries before she found the stone steps that led up to the higher level. Heavily overgrown and very precarious, she was relieved when Harrison took her arm and helped her climb.

Okay, maybe relieved wasn't quite the right word, and maybe she played up her clumsiness a little, especially when his arm went around her waist.

On the last step she stopped and let him take in the scene. A three-meter-high temple, still intact, sat in the middle of a series of rice paddies. Surrounded by the lush green terraces, the ancient building stood tall and proud. How many peasants had planted rice in its shadow? How many had sought blessings or forgiveness from the god worshipped there?

What Jade sought wasn't going to be granted by any temple. Unless there was a god who specialized in people who leaped before they looked. She'd believed all of Keith's lies, uprooted her life to chase him halfway around the world, only to discover he was a lying bastard.

And now she was enticed by a man who had more secrets than the CIA. Maybe she needed to say a quick prayer asking for her to come out of this week with her heart and soul intact. Because as much as she kept telling herself she was spending time with Harrison to help him heal, she was becoming more than just physically attracted to him. He was a man like no other, and she didn't want to miss this opportunity to be with him. Sure, he'd be the one who got away. But while she had him… Well, maybe she'd spend some time fixing herself.

"This is incredible," Harrison said next to her, his voice full of awe. "How come this place hasn't been put on the tourist map?"

"Don't you think the people of Bali deserve something just for them?"

He turned to her then. "Absolutely. I'm honored

that you thought to share this with me."

"You're welcome. Do you want to go closer? There's some intricate carving on the base."

She took a step toward the raised path that skirted the edge of the rice field, but he put a hand on her arm.

"No. This is close enough." His hand slid down her arm until his fingers laced with hers. "This is enough."

His hand in hers unleashed a tempest in her belly. "What about a photo?"

He let go of her hand and raised his camera to his eye but lowered it without pressing the shutter button. "What I want to do … is kiss you." He said it without looking at her, his eyes still focused on the temple.

"Um, okay?"

He turned then. His hand snaked into her hair, bringing her face up to his. His lips, when they met hers, were almost worshipful. The kiss lasted barely a minute, but when he raised his head again, she couldn't have told him what day it was.

This man was either a ninja kisser able to render her incapacitated with one sweep of his tongue, or he was her gateway drug. One hit and she was addicted. Either way, a sensible woman would stay well clear.

Then again, *sensible* wasn't even in her vocabulary. She pulled his head back down for another kiss, needing to make an accurate diagnosis. This time his kiss was less reverential, more conquering. Hastings, Waterloo, the Alamo … every battle that she'd been forced to learn about in school was nothing compared to the complete collapse of her defenses.

If he asked, she'd strip naked right there and let him take her among the rice paddies. But he didn't ask. He was too much of a gentleman.

Dammit, anyway.

This time when he broke the kiss, he stepped away from her. His chest heaved as he pulled in each breath, and there was a discernible bulge in the front of his shorts.

"That's enough sightseeing for today," he said.

With one last long look at the temple, he held out his hand and waited while she put hers in it, then led the way back down the stairs. She slipped once, and he wrapped his arm around her but released her as soon as she'd regained her footing.

When they were finally back to the main site, he strode over to where they'd left the backpack, and drained an entire bottle of water. He wiped his mouth with the back of his hand and checked his watch. "The sun will set in less than an hour. We'd better get down the mountain."

Trust Harrison to turn a passionate moment into a health and safety advisory.

She picked up the backpack and moved toward the edge of the clearing. When she looked back to make sure Harrison was behind her, he still stood where she'd left him, scanning the temple area.

"I thought you wanted to leave," she called out.

After a moment, he hurried over to her. But still he said nothing as they returned to the Jeep.

She backed out of the parking area then glanced over at Harrison. She really had to stop kissing him against his will. At least he'd asked her first.

"Seems I've upset you again," she said.

He ran a hand through his hair. "No. But we have an explosive chemistry that it would be better to diffuse than ignite."

"Why?"

"Because we work together."

"Only for a few days. And then it's not as if we'll see each other again and have any awkward moments."

"Exactly. Why bother exploring this when it can't go anywhere?"

"Haven't you ever had a holiday fling?"

His laugh was bitter. "I've rarely taken a holiday."

"Then this would be perfect for you. I won't tell anyone if you don't." The more she considered it, the more cathartic it seemed. She hadn't been with anyone since the lying bastard. And the "explosive chemistry" she shared with Harrison was definitely hot enough to obliterate any memory of Keith's hands on her body. Vegetation regrew after a bush fire. Sex with Harrison could be the conflagration she needed before reseeding her love life.

She could feel his eyes on her, but as she was navigating a series of tricky turns, she didn't dare glance his way.

"I'll take your offer under advisement," he finally said.

That was so typically Harrison, she laughed. "You do that."

He was quiet for a few more minutes. "Thank you

for showing me the ruins. They were amazing. I had no idea a place like that existed."

"I'm glad you enjoyed it. Do you trust me now to show you a good time?" She darted a glance his way as the road straightened for a minute. He'd undone a couple more of his buttons, and his arm rested on his propped-up knee. It was the most relaxed she'd seen him. Maybe Bali was working its magic.

His smile was full of mischief. "I'll concede that you've surprised me. And I'm willing to have an open mind about anything else you might suggest."

She laughed again. She did that a lot with him. "I forgot you were once a lawyer." At his raised eyebrow she added, "I read your bio on your website."

"I'm still a lawyer."

"How about for the rest of the day, you concentrate on being a man."

"That, Jade, is never in doubt."

She glanced at him quickly again. No, it wasn't— her only doubt was if he'd act on that lustful gaze that lingered on her bare thighs. Heat flooded her core and she shifted in the driver's seat.

"How 'bout we stop for supper before we get back to town? I know a nice little café. Mostly locals eat there though, so it's not fancy."

"Works for me."

The restaurant was owned by a relative and she occasionally brought clients here. The food was excellent and authentic, and Harrison seemed to enjoy it as much as their more expensive dinner the night before.

It was dark by the time they finished, and traffic slowed to a crawl as soon as they got near the town. After not moving for five minutes, poor Sherman started to overheat and kept stalling. Finally, about a mile from their hotel, she couldn't get it started again and Harrison helped her push the vehicle into a parking spot on a side road.

"Sorry, looks like we have to walk from here," she said. "Or we can get a taxi. But the traffic's not moving at all, so it will probably be faster to walk."

"Walking's good. I ate so much; a little exercise will do me good."

That just drew her eye to his flat stomach. The exertion of pushing the Jeep in the heat had made his shirt cling to his body. She'd bet her shoe collection he had a six-pack under the thin cotton. Close, but still untouchable.

"How about we get a drink?" Nothing like a little alcohol to loosen inhibitions. His, not hers. If hers were any looser, they'd be dragging behind her, tethered only by a thin strand of self-respect. The man's nearness did things to her that both thrilled and terrified. It was a first for her, having to convince a man to take her to bed. Her body was usually all they wanted.

At his nod, she led him down a nearby street to a bar well-known for its entertainment. She was so aware of him, her body ached for some skin-on-skin contact. A little distraction would be a good thing.

The place was packed, but they managed to find a table near the stage. Six stools were set up, four of them already occupied by two men and two women. Poster boards and markers sat on the remaining two empty seats.

The bar hostess raced up to Jade and Harrison as soon as they sat down. "Brilliant," she said, her British-accented voice carrying over the music. "We need a third couple to join the game. We've been waiting for ten minutes. Help a girl out, please. The crowd is getting restless. Players get free drinks for the night," she added at the end as an inducement.

Jade looked around the room. Most of the tables were occupied by either groups of guys or girls, there didn't seem to be any other pairs in the room, except for the ones already on stage.

"What kind of game?" Harrison asked.

"The newlywed game," the hostess answered.

"We're not—" he argued.

"Come on, petal, this should be fun." Jade stood and stepped up onto the stage.

Harrison remained next to the table where they'd sat, staring at her like she'd just stripped naked in front of the crowd. Part shock, part admiration.

She challenged him with her eyes, relief flooding through her as he mounted the three steps. He strode over and pulled her flush against his body, his lips grazing her cheek before he whispered into her ear. "You owe me for this. And I will dictate the terms of repayment."

This was so going to be worth it.

Chapter Eight

The stage lights blinded him, and a sheen of perspiration broke out on his forehead. Thank God he'd never see any of these people again. Jade was going to pay for this—preferably naked and submissive. His fantasies from the temple ruins flooded his mind and he shifted on the stool.

The hostess had a scratchy microphone and was running through the rules of the game. She would ask a question, then each couple would write down their answers on the cardboard provided. The couple with the most correct answers would win. He took another swig of the whisky the hostess had brought to him.

The women and men were separated by a rolling blackboard, so he couldn't see Jade. But when they were alone…

Since she'd mentioned the idea of a holiday fling, he'd had a hard time thinking of anything else. He'd never before met a woman quite like Jade: smart, funny, caring, quirky, mischievous, and so damn sexy she stole his breath with a mere laugh. Maybe it was time he looked to the future. Well, at least that small snippet of it that started once he'd finished his business and ended when he had to fly home.

"Okay, couples, here's your first question," the hostess announced. Harrison poised his marker above the cardboard answer card. If he was going to play, he might as well play to win. "What day of the week did you first meet?"

Easy, as it was only two days ago. He wrote *Sunday* on his card and took another sip of the whisky and let linger in his mouth a minute. Jade has ordered the spirit as well, and he imagined the taste on her tongue as he kissed her. Like she'd done to him at the edge of the rice paddies. He'd started it, but she'd taken it to another level. Any control he had with the woman had eroded faster than a sandcastle standing against a tsunami.

"Next question…" The hostess ran through a bunch of questions that a couple would probably know but for him were just guesses: favorite color, favorite drink, favorite flower/sports team, name of best friend, how long respective parents were/are married… The idea of victory faded and he settled for not embarrassing himself.

A full glass replaced his now empty one and he swallowed another mouthful.

A giggle preceded the next question: "What is your favorite sex position? And underneath that, write your partner's."

Harrison's pen froze in his hand. That was a telling question. Jade would undoubtedly write down missionary for him, and his urge to win battled with his desire to see her face when he wrote down the true answer. Desire won and he scribbled his response. He closed his eyes for a second, picturing Jade's answer, and wrote down the one he thought she'd write.

After that, the questions got more risqué and outrageous. About her: nipple color and breast size— he got to choose from "perky," "adequate," and "in heaven." For him, penis size was gauged as "adequate," "impressive," and "oh my God, is that another limb?" What the hell, it was only a game. He wrote his answers as he wished them to be.

The hostess called an end to the game and his drink was refilled again. The blackboard was rolled away, and for the first time in half an hour, he saw Jade. Her tanned skin was lightly flushed and a blaze of desire glowed in her eyes. He was having a difficult time remembering that she was technically his employee and any affair they embarked on had to wait until that status changed.

"Okay, let's check out the answers and find our winner," the hostess said over the mic. There was a smattering of applause and cat calls from the audience, and he took the opportunity to glance over at Jade. She seemed supremely confident, as usual. Except this time, it didn't feel like an act.

They got the day of their meet correct, and favorite color. Hers was blue, and she'd written "like his eyes" in brackets. His was green, and he'd also written "like her eyes" in brackets. That earned them a groan for corniness from the audience. She correctly guessed whisky as his favorite drink, which wasn't too surprising as he'd ordered it twice and told her about his whisky war with Caleb. He guessed wrongly that white wine was her favorite, when it was strawberry margaritas. They both answered correctly for their best friends' names, but got it wrong with their parents' anniversary count.

He could sense the renewed interest in the audience as they got to the personal questions. Favorite sex position. He glanced over to see the answer written on Jade's card for his favorite and was shocked to see "doggy style" written in answer. Correct. There was a titter from the audience when the other couples got it wrong. For her favorite, he'd guessed "cowgirl" incorrectly—she'd also written "doggy style." That she liked to be dominated thrilled him, and his cock jerked in response.

They got one hundred percent on the rest of the answers. Given her coloring, it hadn't taken too much guesswork that her nipples were brown, and he'd already felt her awesome breasts pressed against his chest twice, so he knew they were heavenly. That she'd generously estimated the size of his cock warmed him. Right now, it felt like another limb, and he had to adjust his posture on the chair.

Unfortunately, after all the questions, they were tied with another couple for the win. While the hostess and bar owner came up with three tie-breaking questions, Jade popped off her stool and came to stand in front of him. She straddled his legs, her inner thighs pressing against his outer ones. He could smell the whisky on her breath as she leaned in to talk to him.

"Can you believe we tied for first? The other couple has been married for three years."

"It's probably because our acquaintance is recent, so we remember all these things."

"Except that peonies are my favorite flower, not roses."

"Well, I haven't had any reason to send you flowers yet, so it hasn't come up."

She crossed her arms. "And what constitutes a flower-sending occasion in Harrison Mackenzie's world?"

"A night that redefines pleasure."

She wedged herself closer and ran her hands from his shoulders into his hair as she tilted his face up. As her lips descended, she whispered, "Then you'd better remember: peonies—preferably white ones with hints of pink at the center."

She brushed her mouth against his briefly before the hostess remounted the stage and Jade had to return to her stool.

God, he hoped his brain still had enough function left in it to remind his hand how to hold the marker. What Jade did to him was off the charts. The seize-the-day guy inside, who hadn't had his voice listened to in fourteen years, screamed at him to take what she so blatantly offered and enjoy. The man he'd become since his wife's and son's deaths cautioned that Jade was a bright, beautiful woman inside and out who shouldn't be tarnished by his darkness.

"All right couples, we've got three questions. If we're still tied at the end, we'll have a kiss-off."

Seize-the-day guy liked the sound of that.

"First question: what is your favorite body part on your partner, and what would they answer about you?"

His response was easy, but he had no idea what

part of him Jade might like best. They could always have the kiss-off in private.

"Second question: What's your partner's tell that they're in the mood? What's your tell?"

He heard Jade giggle on the other side of the divider and smiled as he wrote his own answer.

"Final question: What song best describes your sex life?"

Damn, that one was hard. The hostess called time and rolled back the screen again. Jade looked smugly satisfied.

"All right, couples. Show your answers to the first question about body parts."

Unsurprisingly, he'd written breasts, and she'd guessed he'd say that—probably because of the amount of time he'd spent staring at hers when he didn't think she was looking. She'd written that his lips were her favorite part of him, and thankfully, modesty made him write that as well. The other couple got their answers correct, too. The man next to him fist-bumped Harrison, since they'd both written breasts.

"Second tiebreaker question was about how to tell when your partner is horny. Answers please, couples."

The audience burst into laughter when Jade lifted her card. She'd written "he's breathing" and "I'm breathing" as her answers.

They got one point, because he'd also written down "breathing" as his tell. But for her he'd put, "She jumps on my lap." They were still tied with the other couple. The kiss-off, whatever that was, was looking more likely.

"Okay, it all comes down to this. What song describes your sex life?"

He flipped over his card and waited for Jade's reaction. He'd written "Dangerous Woman." She'd written "Feels Like the First Time."

The other couple had both written "Loving You, Loving Me" and were proclaimed the winner. Jade didn't wait for them to be presented with their prize before she leapt on his lap, nearly knocking him off his stool.

Losing had never felt so good.

Her hands cupped his cheeks and her forehead met his. "That was fun," she said. The whisky was stronger on her breath now. He hoped to hell she wasn't drunk, because he couldn't take advantage of a drunk woman no matter how badly he wanted her or how soft and pliable she was in his arms. Sober consent, or the clothes stayed on. It was his number one, unbreakable rule. Jade may have made him forget the others, but that one was inviolable.

"Let's get you back to the hotel," he said, lifting her from his lap before the audience got more of a show than they'd paid for.

"I thought you'd never ask."

The hot, sultry air hit him as they exited the bar. Even at ten thirty on a Tuesday night, Bali bustled with an energy that reminded him he wasn't twenty any more. He felt ancient at thirty-two.

"How old are you, Jade?"

She had an arm around his waist, and his had

naturally settled on her shoulders.

"Twenty-six. Why?"

"Sometimes, you seem much younger. You approach everything with such enthusiasm."

"I guess I learned early that there are no guarantees in life and each moment should be enjoyed because you may not get another."

A baby wailed from a house nearby, delivering an abrupt reality check to his lust-hazed body. Icy memories dug their sharp talons into his desire. "What if enjoying the moment results in more heartache than joy?"

She stopped walking and turned to him. "Then you pick up the pieces and move on. We've all been hurt before, Harrison. But letting the wound fester doesn't help anyone. Let Bali into your heart. You'll be amazed at the difference."

Bali wasn't the issue. It was the woman who currently had one hand on his chest, the other on his cheek. He'd already destroyed one lover. He couldn't risk doing it with another. He wasn't on holiday. He shouldn't have an affair.

Seize-the-day guy wept.

***

Jade's frustration was still on full boil the next morning as she got ready for the day's site visit to the silk screener's. There had to be something wrong with Harrison. What man had a hot, willing woman in his arms and saw her safely to her hotel room before closing the door and going to his own bed? She thought she'd broken through his defenses yesterday, first with the visit to the temple site and then with the newlywed game in the bar.

That he'd participated in the game and even been a good sport with his answers had surprised the hell out of her. That she'd been ready to jump his bones the second they got someplace private had been blatantly obvious. That he'd turn down her offer of a nightcap in her room, saying they had work in the morning, had been annoying as hell. Evidently, he had reserves of self-control she'd not discovered and destroyed yet.

She wound her hair up into a tight bun, slipped on her shoes, and straightened her skirt. Professional Jade was back in charge, and if it killed her, she'd keep her hands off Harrison. The next move had to come from him. She was done chasing.

When she got to the reception area, two men from the silk-screening company were waiting, but there was no sexy, infuriating Canadian in sight. Her phone *pinged* with a message. He was stuck on a call and would be down as soon as it was over. He asked her to pass on his apologies.

Twenty minutes lapsed before Harrison strode into the lobby. His face was like stone. One hand was fisted, and the other clenched his briefcase like it was a weapon. Yet when he greeted her and the men, he was pleasant and charming. Only the tight line around his lips indicated that he wasn't happy.

"I apologize for keeping you waiting. Are we ready to go?" he asked.

"In just a minute," Jade answered. "Can I have a private word with you?"

"Of course."

While she excused herself from the other men, Harrison glared at them. They moved to the other side of the room and he put a hand on her back as they stepped away. The warmth of his touch spread through her. *Down, girl.*

"Have they been rude to you?" His gaze slid past her shoulder to the men who still sat across the room.

"No, not at all." She hurried to reassure him. "They're very nice, family men. I like them."

"So what's the problem?"

"You."

"Me?"

"Something's upset you, and I want to know what it is."

"Just something back home. A personal matter. Nothing for you to worry about."

"Are you sure?"

He stared at her for a moment, his eyebrows drawn together. "You're my translator, Jade. Not my wife or my shrink."

His words stung, and she took a step back. "Sorry if I overstepped. I thought we'd got to the point of being friends."

Without waiting for a reply, she strode back to the managers and advised them that they were now ready to go.

The two-hour drive to the factory was like icing on a meatloaf. It all appeared pretty and pleasant, but underneath was not a fluffy pound cake. Jade darted looks at Harrison, but aside from an occasional question about something they passed, which she dutifully translated rather than answered, he was quiet, clearly still absorbed in whatever had transpired during his phone call this morning.

The workshop was small but clean and neat. A dozen worktables were set up with women silk screening at speeds that made Jade dizzy. But there was a happy buzz within the room, and when they entered, the workers stopped to greet them with smiles.

The smell of paint hung heavy in the air. Two lazy ceiling fans did little to dissipate the chemical fog. Were the women content? Or high? Jade swayed on her heels until Harrison put out an arm to steady her. But as soon as she'd regained her equilibrium, he removed his support. A chill coursed down her spine despite the hot-as-hell temperature.

Whatever they'd once had between them was gone. Jade took a swig of water to try and fill the empty void that had suddenly appeared in her abdomen.

A separate workstation had been set up to one side of the floor, and Mr. Basna led them over to it. A young woman wearing a white smock to cover her jeans and T-shirt then ran them through the process they had been using to put on the various shades of paint in the designs sent over from Canada. Jade translated but added no further commentary. Harrison rarely looked at her, his concentration entirely on the worker. When the process was complete, they were taken to a small storage room that had obviously been cleared out for their arrival as cans of paint, thinner, and other chemicals and tools were neatly stacked against the wall.

With the two managers, Harrison, and Jade inside, the room was claustrophobic. Harrison stood right behind her. His body heat and cologne were even more potent than the paint fumes in the other room. She forced her knees to remain locked and not to lean into him.

Mr. Basna turned off the lights, and the room plunged into darkness. Could Harrison feel her wanting him? Without light, the rest of her senses sharpened, heightening her awareness of him. He took a half step to one side and his thighs brushed against her arse. Good thing the fumes weren't as strong in here, or they could've started an explosion with the spark generated by the touch. Why did her body have to want him? He was way too moody for her.

A black light was turned on, and the T-shirt that lay on the table glowed. But the design was indistinguishable. Some of the paint had adhered to the fabric, but parts of it hadn't. Harrison released a silent sigh that slid down her nape like a caress. She managed to suppress the shiver it evoked, knowing he'd be able to feel it.

The door opened, and the two Indonesian men filed out. Harrison, though, moved over to the table to feel the material. "Do you not wash the shirts before you apply the paint?" he asked.

Mr. Basna turned around and rejoined them. "No. We were assured the fabric was virgin and had not been chemically treated." Jade translated the exchange.

Harrison felt the shirt once more. "I'll take that up with the garment manufacturers tomorrow. To test my theory, please wash one of the shirts and then apply the paint. I want to see if it makes a difference."

"Yes, sir," Mr. Basna replied after Jade translated Harrison's instructions. "In the meantime, we would be pleased to show you some of the sights in our local area."

Harrison nodded, and they piled back in the minivan and were driven along the coast. They stopped at several viewpoints, and although Harrison dutifully took photos with his phone, Jade could tell he was distracted and not really interested. Should she suggest they go to a nearby historical site that he might prefer? Or just leave him be?

Lunch was an elaborate affair in a nearby hotel. Between Mr. Basna and the other manager, Mr. Gatra, she was kept too busy translating to eat much. Not that she minded—she wasn't very hungry.

By the time they returned to the plant, Jade had a massive headache and had to force herself to step into the fume-infested factory.

"The washed shirt has been painted, and although not completely dry, the results are much better." Jade repeated the information from the woman who appeared to be the floor manager.

Once again, they were ushered into the small,

dark storage room. This time, however, Harrison put an arm around her shoulders and tucked her body against his. The overhead lights were extinguished and the black light turned on. Jade gasped at the beautiful image on the shirt. It was almost like a hologram on fabric, showing different designs depending on how the light hit it.

"It's amazing," she said.

Tension bled from Harrison's body, and for the first time that day, he relaxed. His arm shifted from her shoulder to her waist, and she was pretty sure he pressed a brief kiss to her hair.

"I'm glad that mystery is solved. We'll meet with the T-shirt suppliers tomorrow and get the chemical-free shirts delivered immediately. How soon will you be able to have them printed?" Harrison kept his arm around her as they exited the dark room, and she translated his question.

"If the new shirts can be delivered by Monday, we can still meet the deadline," Mr. Gatra replied through Jade's translation.

"Excellent."

The trip back to the hotel was better. Harrison asked about the men's families and related bare bones about his own. She discovered he had a younger sister who was unmarried and worked with their father. The rest she already knew from his bio: he lived in downtown Vancouver and liked rugby. None of it gave any clue as to the fascinating man she'd glimpsed previously.

It was almost six by the time they got back to the

hotel. Jade's stomach had been rumbling for the last half hour.

When the two men finally left to return to their homes, Harrison turned toward her. "Are you free for dinner tonight?"

"That depends. Arc you going to tell me what this morning was all about? I'm not in the mood to have my head snapped off again."

He ran his fingers through his hair and then took her hand in his. "I apologize for that. My father has had another stroke. When I get back to Canada, it looks like I'm going to have to run his company until my sister is better equipped to take over. I shouldn't have taken my family worries out on you."

"Will your dad be okay?" If something happened to her father, she'd be on a plane now, not mucking about with some T-shirts that glowed in the dark.

"I believe so. He was treated very quickly following his collapse. I was going to return straight away, but my mother says there's nothing I can do at the moment and rushing to my father's side will only make him worse. Evidently, he's not being a very good patient and hates that everyone is fussing around him. My sister is handling the business for now, and Caleb is on hand to assist her if needed. But I'm still worried, and I'd rather not be alone tonight. Will you eat with me?"

No way could she refuse him now. The question was: would tonight end as last night had—with both of them in separate beds?

Chapter Nine

The wind from the helicopter rotors whipped Jade's hair against her face and lifted her skirt to indecent levels. Good thing she'd put on underpants tonight.

"Where are we going?" she shouted above the noise. Mercifully, the medication she'd taken for her headache had dulled it to an annoying pressure.

"It's a surprise." To be heard, he'd but his lips right next to her ear, and his warm breath slid straight down her cleavage.

Once inside the chopper, they put on headphones so they could at least talk to each other without shouting … although she'd quite liked it when he'd had to get close so she could hear.

His eyes slid appreciatively along the length of her legs as she crossed them. When she'd accepted his dinner invitation, he'd told her to dress for a night out she wouldn't forget. She was fairly certain that a not-to-be-forgotten night with Harrison wouldn't include clothes, but she put on a flirty skirt, flat shoes, and a halter top that showed off her bare back. She'd debated the longest on the footwear but finally decided that she liked it when he towered over her. Besides, having spent the day in heels already, her feet were ready for a break.

"You can't pronounce our destination, can you?"

His eyes lit with laughter. "Caught me."

He laced his fingers with hers and looked over her shoulder out the window. Since it was dark, there wasn't much to see, but she'd never been in a helicopter before, so she was making the most of it. She'd arranged flights over the volcano for clients but had never been on one herself. Next time she'd do this in daylight—as if there was a possibility of a next time.

They landed twenty minutes later, but as it was dark except for the illuminated helipad, she was none the wiser as to their location.

A man wearing a batik shirt and sarong opened the door and escorted them down a narrow flight of stairs illuminated by tiny lights set in the stone. She could hear the surf crash against the cliff face and a waterfall somewhere to the right. The smell of night jasmine and frangipani filled the air. She inhaled a deep breath to clear the last remaining paint fumes from her system.

They had to cross a narrow swing bridge before climbing another set of steps. At the top was a flat rock with a table set for dinner, surrounded by a hundred candles in various sizes.

"Welcome to Solossa Island," the local man said. "Enjoy your evening." He bowed and then disappeared.

Rather than approach the table, Harrison took her hand and led her to a semi-reclined chair off to the side. "I noticed you were rubbing your temples this afternoon. So I arranged for you to have a head massage and a reflexology treatment."

At his words, two women dressed in spa uniforms appeared. One placed a cool towel around her face while the other lifted her feet and removed her shoes.

"What are you going to do while I'm having these treatments?" she asked Harrison.

"Pretend I'm the one touching you."

Holy petunias, now she would be imagining his hands on her as well.

By the time the women finished, she was a gooey mess, capable only of flopping into a chair. There wasn't a solid bone left in her body. How the hell was she going to manage all those stairs back to the helicopter?

"Feel good?" Harrison stood over her, and when she opened her eyes, the women were gone and he held two cocktails in his hand.

God, this fantasy is good. How many headache tablets did I take?

"I don't think I can move," she said.

He handed her a hurricane glass filled with a pink liquid, a slice of pineapple on the rim. Then he put an arm around her shoulders and lifted her to a sitting position. "Shall I carry you over to the table?"

She took a sip of the drink. An explosion of tropical fruit tastes delighted her tongue. Definitely a fantasy. Closing her eyes, she willed Harrison's clothes to disappear.

"Jade, are you asleep?"

"Shush, you're supposed to be taking your clothes off," she replied. She took another drag of her drink before opening her eyes again.

Damn, he was still fully dressed.

He held a hand out for her glass. "I'd better take that back until you've had some dinner. You didn't get to eat much at lunch, and these are pretty powerful."

"Touch my drink and you die," she said. Just in case, she sipped again, filling her mouth with the intoxicating beverage. The stars began to spin above her. Man, the galaxy moved fast near the equator.

Harrison's laugh filled the night air and for a second, the crickets stopped chirping. "Dinner is served. Do you want me to feed you here?"

She glanced over at the table. Two silver domes sat where the plates had been earlier. The candlelight danced off the beads of condensation from the water glasses and the silver wine bucket full of ice. Harrison held out his hand again and she swung her legs off the recliner and slipped on her shoes.

"How long was I out?" Whatever his purpose in bringing her here, falling asleep on him was just rude.

"Twenty minutes. I was tempted to let you sleep, but the way your stomach was rumbling, I thought you'd better eat before crashing for the night."

As if on cue, her stomach let out a loud roar. *So ladylike.*

Before she got her hopes up as to the meaning of such extravagance, she needed some clarification. "Why all this? Have you decided in favor of a holiday affair?"

"If you're wondering if this is a prelude to seduction, then the answer is no. I wanted to do something to make up for my abrupt departure last night and my rudeness this morning." He took her hand, easing her thumb from her middle finger before kissing the inside of her wrist. "Jade, in the three days I've known you, you've made me feel things I haven't felt in a very long time. You make me long for more moments like this. You're special, and I wanted to show you that, no strings attached."

Her voice was barely a whisper when she replied, "You went to a lot of effort for tonight. Thank you." The little flutter in her chest could have been the alcohol on an empty stomach or the way Harrison looked at her—as if she was the most beautiful woman he'd ever seen. His words might be saying "no affair," but clearly his body wasn't fully on board for that decision.

"Actually, all I did was call my secretary. She made the arrangements." Harrison shrugged it off. Still, he'd had the idea. When was the last time someone had done something so amazing for her? Not even her ex, Keith, who was supposed to have been in love with her, had been so caring. Then again, an expense like this on his credit card would have alerted his wife. And Jade would have been saved the agony of packing up her life and moving to England only to discover that her man was already married. *Bastard.*

She pulled in a breath, but the tightness in her chest that normally accompanied thoughts of him was gone. That was one hell of a massage. Or was it the Harrison effect? It was hard to think of another man when he was near.

"Will you swear to me that you don't have some woman waiting for you back in Canada?" She swayed lightly and landed against his chest.

"I swear. The only women in my life are my mother and my sister. And they'd both welcome a significant other to join their ranks."

"You think I'm a potential significant other?"

A shadow passed over his eyes and she instantly regretted her words. But before she could apologize, he said softly, "A fling is all I can consider, Jade. I won't marry again."

And she'd promised herself never to put her happiness in the hands of a man again, either. Yet here she was, wanting something, anything, from Harrison Mackenzie. "Noted." She pulled out of his arms and walked over to the table, pleased when she made it without falling. *Go, me.*

As soon as Harrison sat, a waiter appeared out of the darkness and removed the silver domes with a flourish. A delicious-smelling *nasi goreng*, spicy noodles, and chicken satay were revealed. "Bon appétit," he murmured before disappearing into the night again.

Jade looked around. How many others waited in the darkness, watching their every move? A shiver ran down her spine. Harrison noted her unease.

"I can have them all leave. But they're only here to assist. And once we're done with dinner, they'll retreat to the mainland unless I call them."

She nodded. At least the reminder that there were others around should stop her from making a fool of herself. She finished her cocktail and had barely put it down before it disappeared. She wouldn't be surprised if there was someone suspended above the table, just out of sight in the darkness, to remove the plates as soon as they finished.

"You do this often? Whisk women away to remote locations and wine and dine them?"

"Never before in Bali." He flicked his napkin onto his lap and poured her a glass of wine. Out of the corner of her eye, she saw a waiter retreat back into the shadows.

"And in Canada?"

"No."

"Don't you date?" She twirled the noodles around her fork and peeked at him through her lashes while she waited for his answer.

"Not often. My sister is my usual plus-one for business or charity functions I'm forced to attend."

"Are you a monk?" Biting down on her lower lip, she waited for his answer. Maybe her first assessment of Harrison had been correct and he never had sex. It would account for why he'd left her alone last night … and ruined her plans for the rest of the evening.

"No. I'm as red blooded as any man. I'm just more discreet than most. And any woman I do sleep with knows up front that's all there will ever be to the relationship."

Well, she'd been told. Forewarned was forearmed. It suited her purposes, since she wasn't looking for a long-term relationship either. Only dammit, he made her wish for one. Until she'd stared into his endless blue eyes, she hadn't known that deep down, she longed to be treasured. To be the first and last thought a man had each day. But while many men had wanted her body, none had wanted her soul. Harrison didn't either. And that stung.

Still, she wanted him. *Double dammit.* What was it with her and impossible men? Would her attraction compass always point in the direction of the unattainable?

"The food is excellent," she said. Blatant subject change. Next time, she'd definitely eat before drinking.

"Try the wine, it's my favorite," Harrison said.

"Are you sure I should be drinking?" But she picked up the glass anyway.

"Don't worry, Jade. I'd never take advantage of you when you're drunk."

And that's exactly why I need to stay sober.

***

Harrison shifted his legs under the table to make more room for his massive boner. God, this woman had him in a constant state of arousal. Weren't you supposed to call a doctor if an erection lasted more than four hours? Or was that only if you'd popped the little blue pill? He certainly didn't need any added stimulus to have it bad for Jade. But neither could he take her up on her offer of a holiday affair while she worked for him.

Honor was perhaps an old-fashioned notion, but he'd been raised to believe it was the defining trait of a man. After the way he'd dealt with Emily, he'd spent the last fourteen years working to regain his standing not only in the eyes of his parents but in his own eyes as well. He wasn't going to jeopardize it now by seducing an employee, no matter how willing she seemed.

Hopefully, tomorrow they'd sort out the issue with the shirts and then he could officially release her from her contract … followed shortly by the removal of her clothes.

For the past twenty-one hours, eighteen minutes, and forty-three seconds—since he'd fled from her hotel room door last night—he'd been telling himself that he had to return to Canada the moment his business in Bali was completed. But staring across the table at Jade, he knew he wouldn't. She'd embedded herself too deeply into his every thought for him to depart without tasting her fully at least once, but preferably a dozen times.

He should never have told his secretary to arrange a romantic dinner for him. It was the first time he'd ever made that request, and clearly the woman had indulged every one of her personal fantasies. Still, the treatments for Jade had been his idea.

"How's your headache?"

"Gone. Thank you for the massage. It was wonderful."

"You're welcome."

"Did you have a treatment as well? You seem a lot more relaxed."

"No. I watched you. Your moans of contentment

were particularly enjoyable."

She put down her fork and trailed her index finger along the back of his knuckles. "Oh, petal, you have no idea how I sound when I'm really enjoying something."

He grabbed his water and drank half of it while Jade laughed. Tomorrow night couldn't come soon enough.

"Why do you keep calling me petal?" he asked.

"It's an Aussie term of endearment." Her eyes sparkled with a wicked gleam. "Besides, I think of you as soft and sweet, so it fits."

With one touch, he could prove to her he was neither soft nor sweet. But if he didn't put a damper on their near-explosive sexual attraction, he couldn't count on her to do it. "Do you still have family in Bali?"

She laughed again at the shift in the conversation. "Heaps. My maternal grandparents, aunts, uncles, cousins, and their spouses and children. Most of them are farmers and live in small villages in the interior. I try to visit every other trip, depending on how long I'm in the country. I don't have much in common with them, but I keep in touch because I imagine that's what my mother would have wanted."

"Will you see them this time?"

"Probably not. I'm contracted with you through Saturday. And then I return to Australia on Sunday, ready to start another assignment on Monday."

"Now that we know the problem, tomorrow should see an end to my need for your services."

She swallowed a large gulp of her wine. "Then I guess Saturday I could go visit them."

He pulled in a deep breath which only filled his head with her citrusy-ginger scent. He already lived with a lot of regrets. If he could help it, he wasn't going to have another "what if" hanging over his head for the rest of his life. "Or we can have forty-eight hours where I'm not your boss and you're not my translator." He raised an eyebrow and waited for her reply, attempting to pretend her answer didn't matter to him.

"Two days, huh? That's not a lot of time for what I'd like to do with you."

"It's all I can offer." It's all he dared to offer. Jade was addictive. He should be in his hotel room right now, helping his sister stabilize his father's business. Sonia was trying to handle everything, but she was fresh out of university and didn't have the practical knowledge to foresee problems on the horizon. But here he was, wining and dining a woman who fascinated him more than he'd thought possible.

"Then I guess I'd better take what I can." She stood and moved over to his chair, then leaned down so her mouth was level with his. "Are you sure we can't start sooner?" The sentence ended with her lips on his, just a nibble before she pulled away. She called out something in Balinese and suddenly the table was surrounded by staff whisking the empty plates away. Only their wineglasses remained.

"What did you tell them?"

"That we were done eating and to wait off-island

until we call."

He stood. "Jade, it would be unethical for me to have an affair with you while you're still technically my employee."

"Then I quit."

That certainly solved the problem.

"And tomorrow?" Soft music floated through the air, and he led Jade to a makeshift dance floor, a canopy of twinkling stars their only companions as the scent of flowers wafted over them on a gentle breeze. He pulled her into his arms while he tried to work out what to do with the impossible woman he held. As they swayed to the tempo, his body offered up all kinds of suggestions.

"Tomorrow, I might find myself in the right place at the right time, able to take on a last-minute assignment to help a Canadian venture capitalist sort out his issues with a local textile company."

He couldn't contain his smile. "How lucky."

She unhooked her arms from behind his neck and undid the buttons on his shirt. He forced his hands to stay on her hips for the moment. This was not a good idea, but for the life of him, he couldn't stop her.

"Hmm, more ink," Jade said, spreading his shirt wide while her hands slipped down his naked chest. "You are a man of surprises."

She wasn't the first woman to comment on his chest tattoo, but her words had the same effect as a bucket of ice water over his head. He hadn't thought about Emily in two days. When staring at the temple in the rice paddy yesterday, he'd been consumed with desire for Jade. Not one thought for the wife who should have been standing beside him.

"Don't." He moved her hand from where her finger traced the outline of the dove in flight.

"Harrison, I…" Her look of confusion ate into his soul.

When the hell would he ever learn? "Jade, this isn't going to happen tonight." He released her and did the buttons back up on his shirt, hiding the tattoo but not its effect. His chest still burned where her finger had been. He needed more time to prepare, to get his emotions firmly battened down. After a sleepless night that he'd spent thinking exclusively of Jade, then the news this morning about his father's latest health scare, he was perilously close to the edge of control. A cliff that Jade could very easily push him over.

As he'd predicted that first night on the beach, she had made him forget. The vows he'd uttered, standing over his wife's and son's graves, were ashes in his mouth.

Anger, tears, a slap to the face—any of those would have been expected, even acceptable reactions to his abrupt announcement. What he got was a gentle kiss on the lips and then Jade sat on the ground at his feet.

"I'm not moving until you explain," she said, crossing her legs like she was getting ready for a long sit-in protest.

"Come on, be reasonable." He reached out a hand to help her up but she just ignored it. "That can't be comfortable."

"Neither is having someone put a needle into your flesh and then inject ink into it. You're not the type of man to decorate your body just for fun. That bird obviously has some emotional meaning for you. Since you didn't want me to touch it, I'm guessing it's got something to do with your wife. Until you tell me what happened to her and why you think you're responsible for her death, I'm staying right here." He could wait her out. She was stubborn, but so was he. "I'm going to sit on this cold, hard rock, hoping that a colony of ants or anything worse doesn't crawl under my skirt…" She gave a dramatic shiver. God, the woman was a diva.

"You have no right to know. It doesn't affect you."

"Yes, it does. We were all ready to get jiggy, then I touch your tat and suddenly I'm the other woman, and you're trying to convince your wife that I mean nothing to you."

Anger and anguish washed though his soul, leaving him shaken. "Jade."

He should leave her here. Return to the helicopter, crawl into his soft, comfortable bed back at the hotel, and have a great night's sleep. She could make her own way back in the morning. But he knew he wouldn't do that. And she knew he wouldn't do that. Stalemate.

Maybe if she knew what a monster he was, she'd no longer want him. Then he could return to Canada and his responsibilities without having to go through Jade withdrawals.

"Fine. But I'm not telling you while you're sitting on the ground. Come lie on the hammock and look at the stars."

Then he wouldn't have to see her eyes narrow in disgust or her lips turn up in a sneer. This time, she took the hand he offered. But rather than walk over to the free-standing hammock set up about ten meters from their dining and dancing area, she wrapped an arm around his waist and gave him a tight squeeze.

"Don't get any ideas about standing next to me while you tell me your story. I'm going to lay with my head on your chest, my arm around your waist, and then we're going to make it all better."

Nothing she could do or say would make it all better. Perversely, however, he wanted to see her try.

Chapter Ten

The hammock swayed slightly as a cool breeze from the ocean flowed over them. As promised, Jade lay with her head on his chest, her arm around his middle and one leg thrown over his as though she wouldn't let him up until she was satisfied with what he had to say.

Why had he reacted to her touching his tattoo? She was a grown woman. He should've taken what she so generously offered and given her a night to remember in return. Then when he stared up at the stars twinkling above him, he'd have a massive smile on his face and not the grimace that currently contorted his features.

They lay in silence for a moment. He liked that she didn't rush him or demand immediate answers. He was still reconciling his body to having her reclined and in his arms with their clothes still on. God, she felt good. They fit together perfectly. It wouldn't be hard to imagine them lying like this for many more nights to come.

"I was a rugby player in high school. Quite good, too. Some of Canada's best universities were scouting me. But my grades sucked." He'd been such a cocky teen, so full of his own importance.

"I can see you playing rugby," Jade whispered. "I bet you were a back. Is that how you got the scar on your forehead?" Her breath slid along his chest, warming him further. Her exotic ginger-citrus perfume and the peachy scent from her shampoo filled his head, banishing some of the darkness.

"Yes. It was only a few stiches but done by a junior doctor, so it left a mark. And fly-half was my usual position. My father, while supportive of my athletics, wanted me to have a proper career and education to fall back on for when my rugby playing days were over. So he insisted that I get my grades up to at least a B or he'd pull me off the team."

"Sounds sensible."

She must have been anxious to know what this all had to do with his wife and her death but seemed content to let him tell the story his way. He had to start at the beginning. Jumping in at the messy end wouldn't be fair to Emily's memory.

"I was in the school library after classes one day, trying to make sense of my math. A girl who sat at the table across from me told me I was doing it all wrong." He'd glanced up into her brilliant blue eyes and immediately thought that with a little makeup, she might be pretty. That his first thought had been about her appearance showed how shallow he'd been. He should have seen the intelligence behind those eyes, the pain, the huge heart that needed to be loved. Protected.

"What was her name?"

"Emily. She was a year younger than me but doing advanced math. She tutored me and got my grade up to a B-plus. Her home life was terrible—both her parents were addicts and her older brother a drug dealer, so she spent most of her time at school … then with me. My mom loved her, my dad thought she was a saint, and my younger sister adored her."

"She sounds wonderful." There was no jealousy or pettiness in Jade's tone. Just admiration for a woman she'd never met.

"She was." He swallowed past the lump in his throat. He could still see Emily's bright face looking at him in adoration: her long, blonde hair pulled up in a ponytail, her pert nose and full mouth begging for the touch of his lips. "In my senior year, school was closed for a teacher's professional development day. My parents were at work, and my little sister was at a friend's house. It was just the two of us. We'd fooled around a bit but Emily was so young, I didn't want to take things too far."

"But that day, you did."

"Yeah. I got a letter in the mail with a scholarship offer to McGill, one of the best universities in Canada—but it was on the other side of the country. Accepting it would mean leaving my family, leaving Emily."

"She must have been so happy for you and devastated at the same time."

"She was, but she put on a brave face. Anyway, I told her that I'd decline, that I'd go to a local school. I was sure the University of British Columbia or Simon Fraser would also offer me something."

Jade nodded, her head rubbing against his chest. Despite the heaviness in his heart, it sent warmth flooding through his system. "I bet she insisted you go to McGill."

"How did you know?"

"It's what I would have done."

Jade and Emily had nothing in common, except maybe this. "She did. I kissed her, and one thing led to another and… It was the first time for both of us."

"You were teenagers in love, at home alone…"

"But I was old enough to know how babies were made. I should have had more self-control. I should've at least used a condom."

"Ah. She got pregnant." No condemnation.

"She wasn't going to tell me. She was going to go through it alone and let me leave for Montreal. But I caught her throwing up one day and dragged the information out of her. Her parents couldn't support her; they could barely stand up most days. And I didn't want my baby raised in that environment, either."

"What about your parents? You said they loved her. Surely she could have lived with them while you were away?"

"You have to know my dad. He's a great guy, but he believes a man must live up to his responsibilities. I got Emily pregnant, so I had to provide for her."

"You gave up your scholarship?"

"Yes, but I graduated with good enough grades to get me into one of the local universities. I applied for part-time studies and got a job in the construction industry during the day. Emily and I got married and rented a basement suite near a high school that had a daycare so new mothers could finish their education.

God, we were both so young—we couldn't even legally drink at our own wedding."

"Your parents refused to help at all?"

"They weren't really in a position to. Dad's company was expanding and there was no spare cash. Mom was working full-time, and my sister was still at home. Besides, I thought I could handle it." He'd still been so full of himself. Positive that he could juggle work, school, and family. Emily had blamed herself, saying she'd ruined his life, when the exact opposite had been true. He'd destroyed hers.

"When did it go wrong?" Jade's hand slid from his waist, up his stomach full of knots to rest over his heart, over the dove tattoo.

"After Bryce was born. Emily had postpartum depression and could barely look after our son. My mom took three weeks off work to help, but couldn't manage to give us any more than that. I quit school but had to keep working, so I couldn't be there during the day. Em's family were no help…"

Jade's muscles tensed and her voice was raw when she asked, "She didn't harm the baby, did she? Or herself?"

"No. She'd never do that. She was so sweet, so gentle. I tried to reassure her, tell her how proud I was of her, that things would get better. But none of it helped."

"Harrison, she had a mental illness."

"I know, but if I hadn't got her pregnant… She'd wanted to be a doctor. I took that dream away from her."

"What happened?"

He was glad she hadn't tried to convince him it wasn't his fault. So many others had, it was like white noise now.

Jade's long, dark hair flowed over his arm and he picked up a strand to feel the silkiness between his fingers. Emily's hair color had hovered been blonde and brown and had the texture of corn silk. Jade's was like liquid petroleum.

"It was a Monday. I woke up at five thirty to get ready to head to the construction site. I checked on Bryce in his cot, surprised but relieved that for once he'd slept through the night—"

Jade sat up, the moonlight showing him her eyes full of pain and compassion. "No."

The horror in her tone was no match for the anguish of finding his three-month-old son cold, his lips blue. It was almost thirteen years later, and the pain still ripped through him.

"Cot death, or sudden infant death syndrome, they call it now." The diagnosis had made no difference. Nor did the number of times doctors and nurses had told him there was nothing he and Emily could have done differently, nothing they could have foreseen. He was the man; it was his job to keep his family safe. He'd failed.

Tears streamed down Jade's cheeks. She'd never seen Bryce or held him in her arms, cuddled his tiny body against her, smelled his sweetness or seen his eyes light up when she'd walked through the door. Still, she wept.

"Emily must have been devastated."

"She was. She blamed herself, saying if she'd been more loving, or held him more, things might have been different. It didn't matter what I or anyone else said, she sank deeper into depression."

"Did she get help?"

"I tried. My parents, even my kid sister, tried to convince her. She refused to see a doctor. I was scared to leave her in the morning to go to work. I paid the neighbor upstairs to check on her every hour."

Jade wiped the remaining wetness from her cheeks with the back of her hand. "You did everything you could. You were grieving your son's death as well. You can't blame yourself."

Logically, he knew that. Guilt defied logic. "After about three months, Emily seemed to get a bit better. She went back to school. I told her that I'd keep working full time so she could go to med school, even move if there was another university she wanted to attend. I actually thought it might be better if we left the area."

Jade nestled back against his chest. She must have known there was more to the story. "How did Emily die?"

"What I'd taken for recovery was her hiding a substance abuse problem. Evidently it started with marijuana she got from her brother, then shifted to crack cocaine. I found her dead on our kitchen floor, on what would have been our son's first birthday."

His shirt was soon soaked with Jade's tears. He wrapped both arms around her as she wept for his son and wife.

There were no more tears left in him to shed.

"I got the dove tattoo the day I buried Emily next to our son."

***

Great, now she had the hiccups. Emotional outbursts always did that to her. As her diaphragm spasmed, Harrison held her. Occasionally his hand would rub up and down her back or he'd press his lips to the top of her head. That he was trying to comfort her only made it worse. Her heart, damn, her whole body ached for him.

As he'd recited his story, she'd felt each brick in the wall around his heart reinforce itself. How could a man love again after that double tragedy?

"It's getting late, Jade. We should get back to the hotel." His voice was soft but emotionless. He sat up, bringing her with him.

"Can we stay here? It's the dry season so not likely to rain. Dawn will wake us, and the helicopter will get us back to the hotel in time for your meetings." He'd started to shake his head. "Please, I don't want to be alone tonight." Without his strong arms around her all night, she'd be picturing him holding his dead son or losing his wife on a day that should have been a celebration. That he was the one comforting her showed how screwed up she was.

"All right. I'll get us some blankets."

A minute later, a man appeared with three

blankets and a basket with toothbrushes, toothpaste, washcloths, and a few bottles of water. "Did you plan to spend the night?" If he did, he undoubtedly expected there'd be a better reason for her not wanting to leave.

"No, not planned. Maybe hoped."

"Harrison—"

"Go to sleep, Jade. I'm too exhausted to do anything else."

He did sound shattered. Recounting his emotional journey must have been hard on him. Hell, she'd only listened to it, and she could barely keep her eyes open.

They settled back onto the hammock. She was glad that Harrison spread the blankets over the two of them rather than giving them each one. She tried to get comfortable next to him but with his greater weight, it was almost impossible not to roll on top of him.

"We're going to have to cuddle." His deep voice filled the night and warmed her better than the covering. He lifted his arm, and she didn't need a second invitation to rest her cheek on his chest. Her hand automatically rested where the dove was tattooed into his skin. Realizing what she'd done, she went to move her palm when Harrison's hand covered hers. "Leave it. It helps."

She shifted her head to try and see his face, and his lips brushed her forehead. "Good night, Harrison. For the record, I think you are an amazing man."

His chest expanded under her and his hand on hers tightened briefly.

The next thing she knew, the bed swung wildly

beneath her. The ink black sky that had been dotted with stars now held the glimmer of a new day on the horizon.

"Sorry, I tried to get out without disturbing you. I need to pee," Harrison whispered.

While he was gone, she brushed her teeth, cleaned her face, and finger-combed her hair. Her eyes met his when he returned, not quite sure how he'd react in the cool light of day.

"Ready to get going? I called the pilot, and the chopper will be ready when we are."

"Yes." She looked around the spot. With the sun inching over the horizon, the area was suffused with a pink glow. Drawing in a deep breath, she let the dawn fill her with hope. Last night had been therapeutic, if not for Harrison, at least for her. After what he'd been through, her broken heart paled in comparison. She would no longer give her ex-boyfriend the power to dictate her future love life.

On the way back to the hotel, they flew over the dormant Kintamani volcano. In the early morning light, the waters of Lake Batur were almost black, contrasting with the white steam from the still-active volcano of the same name. The valley was hung with mist that would quickly disappear once the sunlight hit it. It was magical. If she had her way, it would be a portent for the rest of the day. Harrison had offered her forty-eight hours after his business was finished. Did he still want her after last night? She tried to read his expression, but he stared out at the scenery, his back to her.

Jade held her head high as she walked through the hotel lobby in last night's clothes. The walk of shame was slightly less embarrassing when you returned via helicopter. And when Harrison looked even more rumpled than she did.

"There's a car arranged to take us to the garment manufacturer. I'll meet you back here in ninety minutes, if that's okay? I have a few calls to make, so I'll eat breakfast in my room." He sounded almost apologetic for not sharing the morning meal with her.

"No worries. I'll see you at eight."

A shower, coffee, and breakfast refreshed her body, but her spirit was still battered. However, she plastered on a smile as she joined Harrison in the lobby. His hair was slightly damp, and the cologne he'd applied to his freshly-shaven jaw made her want to lick him all over. The lust that had abated when he'd told his story roared back to life.

"Today's meetings are likely to be acrimonious. I need you to keep alert and translate not only what's said out loud but what might be whispered or inferred. This company is in breach of contract for not providing chemical-free shirts. If I had the time, I'd find someone else, but that's just not feasible at this point. There's a huge festival in a few weeks, and we want to hit that market." He was back to being all business, and she forced herself not to reach up and flatten a piece of his hair that had dared move out of place. That's the sort of thing a wife or a girlfriend would do, not a contracted translator.

"Got it."

The hour drive to the plant was conducted in near silence. Harrison sat up front with the driver and stared out the window for most of the trip. But when they arrived, he opened her door and offered her his hand to help her out of the tall SUV. A gentleman to the end.

They were met at the entrance by three men with their chests puffed out like they owned the world. One of them Jade recognized from a recent documentary on corruption. She pretended to have a stone in her shoe so she could lean on Harrison and whisper the information to him. His arm tensed under her hand. "Stay close to me," he replied sotto voce. "If anything happens, I'll protect you."

With a fake smile pasted on his face, he greeted the men. They embarked on a quick tour of the factory, during which Jade's shoes proved a complete nuisance to the plant managers because she had to constantly stop to whisper translations of what the workers said. She made an exception for those few times when the women were gossiping about how good-looking Harrison was, of course. She didn't consider that vital information.

When they moved into a meeting room, however, the tension in the air increased. Jade sat as close to Harrison as possible, glad for the reassurance of his strong body. Although he kept his voice steady, the other men began to shout, and translating their simultaneous outbursts became difficult. Harrison held up his hand and waited for calm to prevail.

When they walked out an hour later, he'd negotiated for them to remake the entire order of shirts with new fabric of a better quality to make up for the stiffness that had been a result of the sizing chemicals. The shirts were to be delivered to the silk screen printers by Monday morning. Any failure to comply with the terms would cancel the payment and bring a breach of contract lawsuit against them. Jade made sure to clearly translate the implied threat that he would destroy their company.

Back in the SUV on the return to the hotel, Harrison sat in the back with her.

"You were amazing," she said. "I thought one of them was going to wet himself when you threatened to sue for damages. Do you think they'll comply?"

"They'd better. Even if they fully meet our terms, this is the only contract they'll get. We'll source another supplier for future orders. I won't work with people I don't trust."

"I guess this means my time as your employee is also over?" She held her breath, waiting for his reply.

"Yes. Your contract is concluded." He reached over and touched her hand where it rested on the seat between them. "But if you're not put off by last night, I'd like to spend the rest of my time in Bali with you."

The weight on her chest released and she drew in a deep breath. "I'd like that, too. And I know just the place we can go."

"What's wrong with the hotel?" That damn imperious eyebrow was up again, and she had to stop from undoing her seatbelt, straddling him, and kissing that smirk off his face.

Instead, she met it with a haughty stare of her

own. "I want to make lots and lots of noise," she said.

His smile could've melted rock. "Me too." The heat from his gaze incinerated any inhibitions she had left. She just hoped the noise they made wouldn't include the sound of her heart breaking again.

Chapter Eleven

"Where are you taking me?" They were back in Sherman the Jeep, lumbering up a steep mountain. Sheer drop on one side, jagged rock face on the other.

"Haven't you been leaving a path of shiny pebbles?" Jade glanced at him briefly before shifting the elderly vehicle into a lower gear. Her thigh muscles flexed below her shorts and he drew in a ragged breath. Soon he'd sample every centimeter of those golden limbs, then wrap them around his waist and ride her to oblivion. The trick would be to restrict their connection to the physical. Because God help him if she wiggled her way further into his life.

"I did. But then I ran out and my breadcrumbs got soaked in that rain shower we passed through." What he really wanted to know was how much longer he had to wait until he could run his fingers through her glorious ink-black hair, latch his mouth onto her neck, and head south to the promised land.

"Excellent. Then there'll be no trace of where you went. I can keep you as my love slave for as long as I want."

"Hell, if I knew that was your endgame, I'd have packed faster." He'd thrown everything he had into his suitcase in seconds. The call home to check on his father was what had taken the time. At least that had been good news. Harrison wanted the next two days to concentrate on Jade, not field calls from Canada.

She shot him a smile full of lust and he sat back and let the amazing view fill his soul. Well, as much as he could while clinging on to the dashboard for dear life. Finally, the road leveled off, and after five minutes Jade pulled over into a narrow lane just wide enough for the Jeep.

"We're on foot from here," she said.

She had promised him someplace they could make lots of noise. Since the last village they'd passed through had to be at least ten kilometers back, there didn't seem to be anyone around to hear her screams of ecstasy. And he would take her there. Over and over again. Until he had to leave. His chest tightened.

"Can you get the Esky out?" She pointed at a large cooler with wheels before she slung her backpack over her shoulder and reached for his bag. "There's no running water or electricity, so I had to bring enough food and drink for us."

He blinked at her. "You do know I'm a billionaire, right?" It still shocked him when he thought about his wealth. He'd been raised in a family where money was carefully monitored. His father had started his company with nothing but skill and determination, and now it was one of Canada's top ten property development firms. Harrison, while comfortable thanks to his legal career, had hit the ten-figure income bracket with a silly online game that he'd never even mastered. The irony made him laugh. For the first time, however, he wanted to use that ridiculous money to indulge Jade's every whim. "I could hire a private island like I did last night and we could spend our time together in luxury."

"Where's the fun in that?" She dragged his bag behind her and set off on the packed dirt track. The air was cooler with the higher elevation. Still, it was damn hot. And there'd be no air conditioning. This place had better be worth it.

After passing through a few trees, they walked into a series of rice terraces. The path Jade followed wound between the paddies. One false move and he'd be up to his knees in rice, water, and whatever was lurking in the murky depths. Dusk was drawing in. Soon it would be pitch black. He hoped it wasn't far to their destination.

Jade stopped abruptly and he nearly ran into the back of her, just managing to keep the cooler from tumbling into the paddy. Had he been leading, he'd have stopped as well. Before them stood a large wooden structure with a wraparound veranda and a thatched roof. It appeared to perch on the edge of the world, since beyond that, he could see nothing but sky. He couldn't remember ever seeing a more beautiful location for a house.

"Sorry, it gets me every time," Jade said, a note of reverence in her voice.

"What is this?"

"My house. Come on, we need to get settled before sunset."

She hurried on ahead and flung open the door. "This is your house?" He lifted the cooler up the two stairs and followed her into the living space. The home was made of tropical wood, the vaulted ceiling revealing the thatched roof covering. But inside, everything was exquisitely carved, the furniture traditional but comfortable. A sofa swung from an overhead beam on heavy chains.

"Technically, it's my father's house. My relatives own the land around it, but my dad bought this plot and built the house here so they could have privacy when they visited Mum's family or they wanted to get away from the resort they owned. I always loved coming here as a child. Mum used to sing loudly and dance around the room." Her breath caught, as it always did when she spoke of her mother, but her face brightened as she turned back to Harrison. "But since Dad hasn't been here in four years, I've taken over. Wait till you see the best bit."

She abandoned their bags by the door and rushed over to the far wall. She flicked a couple of bolts on the floor and the whole rear wall slid back, revealing the most amazing view over the valley below and the rice terraces climbing the hill on the other side. A small deck seemed to defy gravity and jutted out into the scenery.

He stood transfixed at the view as Jade lit several lamps dotted around the room. When she next came to stand beside him, she handed him a glass of scotch. She touched the rim of her glass to his and then wrapped an arm around his waist as the sun slowly sank over the horizon in a glorious display of oranges, pinks, and magentas. He slung back his drink and then turned to the woman at his side. They were on the clock, and he had so many fantasies to fulfill.

But first, honor demanded that he make sure Jade knew this was all he could ever give her. He lifted her left hand. Sure enough, her thumb and middle finger were pressed together. "Were you aware that *this* is your tell when you're nervous and hiding behind false bravado?"

She separated her fingers, but he kept hold of her hand. "You must be great at playing poker," she said.

"I don't gamble."

A strangled laugh escaped her. "Well, I'm a sure bet. I want you, Harrison. If I'm nervous, it's only because I'm worried about disappointing you."

A sure thing could still wind up costing more than he could afford. "You will never disappoint me. I like you, Jade. I like everything about you. And I'm convinced that you deserve more than me. More than this no-strings, one-off, casual affair. But that's all I can offer."

"And that's all I need right now. I'm not going to lie. One day I want a love like my parents had—one strong enough to move mountains—with a man who wants my soul as well as my body. But I know that's not what we have. All I want is for you to erase the memory of my last boyfriend. I want to experience an all-consuming passion. I want to feel alive."

God, he wanted those last things mentioned as well. Maybe not the boyfriend bit, but he wanted to let his desires have free rein, if only for a day or two.

"Did you bring that dress you wore the first night

in the bar?"

Even in the low light, he could see the flame of desire in her eyes. "Yes."

"Go put it on."

He wandered back into the house to explore while Jade changed. There was a small but neat kitchen in one corner, complete with propane stove and a small sink minus the faucet. A five-gallon plastic bottle sat to one side with a spigot to dispense the water.

But best of all, there was an island with three barstools next to it. He poured another two drinks from the whisky bottle on the counter and waited for Jade's return. Her heels clicked on the wooden floor as she sauntered over to him with extra sway in her hips. Thank God she'd remembered the shoes. Sidling up next to him, she took the glass he offered.

"You're not about to call me a whore again, are you?" There was a breathlessness to her voice that betrayed her anticipation.

"No. I'm about to fulfill every fantasy I've had since I first saw you in that dress on Sunday."

"You wanted me then?"

"Every man in that room wanted you. But I'm the only one who gets to have you. Loosen the ties holding up the top."

"You're bossy," she said but did as he asked. The fabric opened enough so he could reach in and touch her breasts.

"I like to be in charge. Will that be a problem?" With one finger, he repositioned the fabric so her breasts were exposed in the middle, the tension of the ties still fastened behind her neck holding them in place.

"No. But at some point, I will make you lose control," Jade promised.

He ignored that. Many women had tried. They'd given him pleasure, yes, but make him forget who and where he was? Never. But looking at Jade now, her full breasts exposed, her dark nipples already pebbled, waiting for his touch—for the flick of his tongue, to be sucked hard into his mouth—she may just have a chance. He dipped a finger in his glass of whisky and wet her nipples, gratified by her shuddered indrawn breath.

Rather than start there, though, he aimed his lips for her jaw and traced his way along to her ear, nipping and soothing her delicate skin as went. One hand cupped her breast, his thumb rubbing circles around her nipple while the other found the hem of her dress and slid under, up her silken thigh.

"Christ, Jade, you're commando. Do not tell me you weren't wearing panties on Sunday."

"You'll never know." Her words ended on a moan as his finger slid between her thighs. She was already soaking wet.

"What's the highest number of orgasms you've had in one night?"

"Three." Her breath was coming in short, sharp pants, her eyes glazed over with passion.

He could make this fast. Or he could make this good. He was going for incredible. "We're going to blow that number out of the water."

Her hands went to his shirt and she started to unbutton it, but this was his fantasy. "Put your hands behind your back until I say you can touch me," he said. His mouth hovered over her left breast, his fingers still rolling the nipple on her right. As she complied with his command, it thrust her chest against his lips. He didn't open his mouth, waiting for Jade to become impatient. It didn't take long.

"Please, Harrison," she moaned.

His tongue darted out and licked the whisky from her nipple. She was already rocking against his hand between her thighs—a little more pressure, and she'd come. He, however, was a long way from letting that happen. Removing the hand that had been pleasuring her, he grabbed her hips and lifted her onto the barstool. He released the ties at the back of her neck and her breasts sprang free from their confinement. Cupping them both with his hands, he lavished them with attention, licking, sucking, blowing air on them, and nipping gently. Jade's breathing was deep and rapid, but she said nothing.

He tested the sturdiness of the kitchen island before lifting Jade onto the top. "You can use your hands now to hold on," he told her as he spread her legs wide, propping them on two barstools. He pushed her skirt up to her waist to give the same attention to her core as he'd done to her breasts. He thrust his tongue into her while flicking his finger rapidly over her clit. She came with a scream, her whole body convulsing.

"Oh God, Harri!"

He paused as the nickname scraped against the scar tissue of his heart. As she slowly drifted back to earth, he stared at her. Her dress was bunched around her waist, her breasts called to him once again, and her skin was flushed with her orgasm. Strands of her black hair clung to her sweat-dampened face, down her back and over her shoulders. He picked up one piece and used it to tease her nipples.

"Can you stand?"

She nodded.

Lifting her off the island, he stood her in front of her. "Don't move. I have to get a condom."

"I want to taste you first," she said. Without waiting for his reply, she sank to her knees and undid his belt and pants before shoving them and his boxer briefs to his thighs. As her lips closed around him, a moan tore from his throat. He could feel his control slipping, but the urge to regain the upper hand had mysteriously disappeared. Her tongue drove him wild while her hands slipped up and down his inner thighs, pausing briefly to caress his balls before retreating. She took as much of him in her mouth as possible, sucking hard before pulling away to flick the tip of his cock with her tongue. It was the most exquisite torture. Holding onto his hips, she sat back on her heels and looked up at him with a satisfied smile. "And all along, here I thought it was your name that was the mouthful. I was so wrong."

She was about to take him in again when he put both hands on her head. "I have to be inside you. Now."

Finally released, he went to get a condom from his bag, and when he returned, Jade was leaning over one of the barstools, her bare ass in the air, her breasts dangling down. He grabbed them first, pulling at her nipples then rolling them between his fingers. She wriggled backward, trying to make contact again with his cock. Releasing one of her breasts, he slid one, then two fingers inside her. Still drenched from her earlier orgasm, she clenched around him. Unable to resist any longer, he replaced his fingers with his cock. Hauling in a deep breath, he filled his nose and lungs with her exotic scent, heightened by the smell of her sex.

Her tight walls surrounded him, urging him to let go and pound into her until they both found release.

"Hard and fast, Harri." Jade's request was almost his undoing.

"I don't take orders," he growled. To prove his point, he withdrew slowly before inching his way back into her. He did it again and again, varying the speed and depth of his penetration until she was almost sobbing with pleasure.

"Please," she gasped as he filled her once more, wriggling his hips to get every last millimeter of him inside her.

Her plea broke his restraint and he plunged in and out, his thighs slapping into her ass until she screamed on the wave of another orgasm. As she spasmed around him, he gave himself over to the pleasure and rode her until his own climax came.

Jade's knees buckled, and he grabbed her around the waist before she fell.

Fantasy number one was checked off his list. Now on to number two.

***

Daaaaammm. She knew he'd be a good lover, but that had been epic. And from the grin on his face as he carried her effortlessly into the bedroom, he'd had his socks knocked off as well. But not literally. Because he was still entirely dressed, having even pulled his trousers back up before he'd lifted her. It didn't seem fair when her dress was bunched around her waist like a deflated inner tube.

He sat her on the bed then found the hidden zipper at the side of her dress and slid that down before tugging the fabric past her hips. Now she was fully naked, except for her shoes. She reached down to slip off the strappy heels when his gruff voice stopped her.

"Leave them on."

She had a forceful personality and had always held her own in the bedroom. But something about Harrison's commands and the way he ordered her around turned her on. Her clit throbbed, waiting for his next order.

"You're overdressed for the occasion, Mr. Mackenzie." She wanted to call him Harri again, but he'd tensed and paused the last two times she'd done it, and she didn't want to risk having him stop whatever he had in mind for her next. Not when her body, that five minutes ago was too spent to even breathe, had flared to life as his gaze caressed her. But she did want to get her hands on all those delicious muscles.

He pulled his shirt over his head, not bothering with the buttons, then released his trousers, stepping out of them and his shoes and socks. His thick erection pushed against the confines of his boxers.

"You forgot something," she said, reaching out grab the waistband of his underwear.

Instead, his hand grasped her wrist and held it away from him. "Not yet. Push your breasts together."

She complied, wondering what he'd do next. He tweaked her nipples, as though he was adjusting the knobs on an old-fashioned radio. The pleasure-pain sent heat flooding to her core. As if he knew where she felt it, he trailed one finger down her abdomen, circling her navel before positioning it between her slick folds. While his finger circled lazily, he put one of her heels on her shoulder and then kissed and licked his way up her leg to her inner thigh.

By the time his mouth reached where his finger still played, she was writhing. Her hands clutched the bedspread to anchor her body to the mattress. He glanced up at her. "Breasts," he commanded again. "Don't let go until I tell you. I'm coming back for them."

She pushed her boobs together again, her fingers plucking and flicking her nipples as he'd done earlier. Her nerve endings were alive, each sensation like a crest of a wave, taking her higher. And dammit, he wasn't even breathing heavy.

Two fingers slid inside her, his thumb circling her

clit while her second leg joined the first as he hooked her ankle over his shoulder. He repeated the kisses, licks, and nips up her other leg, soothing them with his tongue and lingering on her inner thigh, increasing the pressure of his bites as he neared her core.

He leaned over her, forcing her knees to bend as he proceeded to devour her breasts. Both his hands were playing with her lower body—stroking her, fingers delving in then retreating, circling and pinching her clit. His mouth clamped around one nipple and he sucked hard the same instant three of his fingers penetrated her while he rubbed her bundle of nerve endings with his thumb. She screamed in pleasure, her upper body jackknifing off the bed.

While she was still wracked with spasms from her climax, he licked his way down her body until he'd impaled her with his tongue. This man's mouth on her was every naughty fantasy she'd ever had. Pleasure spiraled again and she rode the crest once more to another shattering orgasm. When the tremors lessened, Harrison propped both her shoe-clad feet on the edge of the bed, her knees bent.

"Don't move."

She closed her eyes as he left the room, too boneless to even raise her head to see where he went. She sensed his presence before he even touched her. He stood next to the bed between her raised knees. His shorts were gone and another condom sheathed him. God, he was magnificent. And after this, she was done playing the silent partner. He had a body she ached to explore.

She made a move to roll over, remembering he liked doggy style best, when he stopped her with a hand on her knee.

"I want to watch your face as you climax this time."

She wanted to watch his face as well, see him lose control. He remained standing beside the bed and put her ankles up on his shoulder again then raised her hips and thrust into her. She'd cooled down as her last orgasm ebbed, but the second his cock entered her, she was on fire again, riding the tide of passion to another climax. There was no teasing, no prolonging the pleasure as long as possible. Harrison slammed into her over and over, the angle of his penetration putting friction on her clit with each stroke. This was a branding. Harrison had claimed her.

The crescendo was no less intense than the previous times, and her voice was raw as she screamed his name.

He followed her over the edge and collapsed next to her on the bed. With the last of her strength, she rolled to her side to stare into his face. He was so incredibly good looking, and the best lover she'd ever had. A man with whom she could easily fall in love. A man who was leaving in less than two days. A man who had blown her circuits four times so far, yet hadn't kissed her on the lips once.

To him, what they'd just experienced was sex. To her, it was so much more. She rolled over so he wouldn't see the tears she could feel pooling. Her heart—the organ she'd thought was too bruised to ever feel again—wrenched, sucking the breath from her body.

Dammit. In trying to fix Harrison, had she broken herself?

Chapter Twelve

A faint light illuminated the eastern horizon. Jade sat crossed-legged on the back deck, waiting for the sun to rise. Of all the days since Keith's betrayal, today she needed to find her center and hold onto it for dear life. She'd bragged to Harrison about how Bali could heal him, but it may have done her in. She was falling in love with a man still hung up on his dead wife.

At least it was a change from loving a man still attached to a live one. How stupid had she been to fall for Keith's charm? She should've known a man that good looking, straight, and wealthy was already taken. But no, she'd believed the bare ring finger and given him her heart, sure he was her soulmate. He had seemed equally smitten, jumping into her bed on their second date. After that, they were almost inseparable for the six months he'd been assigned to his company's head office in Melbourne.

Shaking her head, her mind flitted to another parting. This one had been at the airport, when Keith had promised to keep in touch, saying he'd apply for a permanent transfer to Australia just as soon as a position became vacant. She'd been so trusting, so sure that they'd be together soon. But when six months turned to ten and his phone calls and messages became more infrequent, she'd decided to take things into her own hands. Her parents' marriage had shown that time could be limited, and she wasn't going to waste hers on the other side of the world from the man she loved.

Carpe-ing the crap out of that diem, she'd packed up her life and headed off to England.

The second huge warning sign should have been when he'd met her reluctantly at the airport and taken her to a hotel and not his home. Of course, she'd figured out the truth the next day when she'd followed him from work, sneaked a peek through his lounge window, and found him kissing a woman like a lover, a wedding ring firmly on his finger, then swinging around a toddler who called him Daddy.

The urge to walk up to his front door and confront him about his duplicity had been deep. But her sense of shame had been deeper. Before she could give into her need to kick his arse, she'd gone back to the hotel, taken the next flight home, blocked his number and email address, and sworn never to let another man close enough to hurt her again. Yet here she was, with the same emptiness swallowing her heart that she'd felt from the other side of that window, watching Keith kiss his wife hello.

Clearly, she hadn't learned her lesson about getting emotionally involved. Harrison had wiped the thought of Keith's touch from her body. But nothing short of a nuclear explosion was going to erase the memory of Harrison bringing her to orgasm over and over. He'd done as she asked—he'd made her feel alive. But would she ever feel this amazing again?

Placing the back of her hands on her knees, she

closed her eyes and searched for inner peace ... although right now, she'd settle for the ability to say goodbye to Harrison tomorrow while retaining some of her dignity.

Last night had been incredible. After his command performance bringing her to climax four times in quick succession, they'd cooked a meal together—well, heated up what she'd brought—and fed each other. They had a few more drinks, talked dirty, and finally kissed—a long lip-lock that had reassured Jade that for Harrison as well, this was more than just casual sex.

But her life was in Australia, his in Canada. No way in hell was she uprooting herself for another man only to end up heartbroken. Besides, he'd said this was all he could offer. And she'd agreed to his terms. He hadn't lied or led her on. This emotional quagmire was all her own fault.

Harrison would be the one who got away. *Queuing Katy Perry earworm.*

The *creak* of the wooden floorboards told her she was no longer alone. She opened one eye and glanced over at Harrison, who had taken up a pose similar to hers.

"Mind if I join you?" His deep voice rumbled through the quiet dawn air.

She nodded, not trusting what might come out of her mouth unfiltered. But his presence completely destroyed any peace she'd managed to achieve. Even with her eyes closed, she was very aware of every breath he took. The blood seemed to race faster on the side of her body closest to him. She began to sway and had to open her eyes or risk toppling over.

"You're not supposed to think about sex when you meditate," she said.

His eyes popped open, a wicked grin lifting his lips.

"How did you know I was thinking about sex?"

She ran a crimson polished finger across the front of his boxers, where his erection tested the fabric's stretch limits.

He chuckled. "Busted. But you shouldn't meditate wearing only a see-through white wrap. Are you finished, or do you want me to go inside?"

Even then, she'd know he was waiting for her. And based on the dampness between her thighs, inner peace wasn't going to happen anytime soon.

"Stay. But let's talk." The sex had been so frantic last night that they'd barely spoken, aside from his commands. And during dinner, she hadn't wanted to break the orgasmic spell cast over them.

He stretched his legs out in front of him. "What do you want to talk about?" His relaxed stance was belied by the wariness in his tone.

"Did Emily call you Harri?" God, why had she asked that? They had only hours left together, and she'd resurrected the dead wife. She glanced over, sure his hard-on would shrivel before her eyes.

"No. I've never liked the shortened version of my name, so I refused to answer to it. Until now."

"Do you mind if I call you Harri?"

"Not when your lips are also doing other things."

In other words, as long as they were having sex, she could call him whatever she wanted. She stared out at the view. The sun caressed the valley now. Another day had begun.

When she glanced back at him, he stared at her as though trying to memorize every aspect of her being. Warmth flooded through her. Before she blurted out something stupid, like "don't leave me," she needed to know what he felt about the future. "What do you want from life?"

"For my family to be healthy and happy and to do some good with the money I have." He stated it with practiced ease, as if it was something he'd been trying to convince himself of for years.

"You don't want to marry again, have more children?"

He was quiet so long, she didn't think he'd answer. Finally, he said, "I can't. Emotionally. If something went wrong… I couldn't endure it again."

"That's a shame." She closed her eyes and tried to concentrate on letting go of the pain. It was ridiculous. She'd gone into this affair knowing it was just a bit of fun before they both went back to their lives. But something had shifted when he'd told her about Emily and Bryce. And the walls she'd thought she'd put up around her heart had completely tumbled when he'd said she deserved more than him. No man had ever thought he wasn't good enough for her. Especially not a man as amazing as Harrison. She'd agreed to the no-strings affair, thinking that it would be enough to be the woman who brought Harrison back to life.

But now, dammit, she wanted to be the one who got to keep him, as well.

"Jade..." His voice was rough—a warning to himself, or her?

In the few minutes they'd been talking, a big black cloud had crept over the house, obliterating the little bit of light that had broken through with the dawn. A fat drop of rain hit the part of the deck not covered by the roof, soon followed by another.

"Come on. This is our chance to shower."

She stood and rushed out into the rain, getting soaked in seconds. Lifting her face to the sky, she let the deluge disguise the tears that slipped from her eyes.

"You're kidding me, right?" The water sluiced down his golden body, rippling over the muscles she'd traced with her tongue and lips the night before. It was an amazing sight.

"No running water, remember? Follow me." She led him across the deck to the side of the house where an area had been screened off with walls on three sides. A small shelf held soap, shampoo and conditioner. Unwrapping her cover-up, she threw the material over the top of the wall and grabbed the soap.

Harrison took it from her. "Allow me," he said rubbing the bar between his hands. He lathered her body, the slippery soap heightening the touch of his hands on her. When his fingers slipped into her heat, a low moan escaped her throat. This is what they had. Intense chemistry but nothing else. At least on his part.

"You always shower with your underpants on?"

She ran her finger around his waistband, encountering his erection. He sucked in a breath.

"We're outside."

"And no one is around. I didn't think you were a prude."

"Last night should have proved I'm not. What I am is private."

Putting her hand inside his pants, she slid a soap-covered palm along his hard-on. "Let go, Harri. You're not likely to have an opportunity like this again."

His reply was a growl, but he shucked his boxers and then stood like a proud Greek statue. Not even the cool rain diminished the magnificence of him fully aroused.

She picked the soap up from where he'd dropped it on the floor and proceeded to lather him as he had her. The rain swept the bubbles down the drain and away from the rice paddies.

When they were both delirious with desire, he lifted her against the wall and impaled her with his shaft. She wrapped her legs around his waist and reveled in the pounding of his pelvis against hers. There was no finesse in his thrusts, no teasing withdrawal and retreat that had characterized their earlier loving. This was fierce. Unrestrained. And she loved it. Finally, she'd broken through his reserve and made him lose control. Her orgasm was fast and furious, sweeping through her like a tornado, wiping everything from her mind but the feel of Harrison inside her.

He threw his head back and roared as he released inside her. Still, he kept pumping until she screamed as a second climax left her boneless. She didn't even have the strength to unhook her legs from his back. He rested his forehead against hers until his breathing evened out.

Suddenly, he stiffened. "Shit. I didn't use a condom."

"I'm clean." When his muscles didn't relax, she added, "And on the pill. I won't get pregnant."

"Thank God."

Why did she just feel like she'd been stabbed in the heart? She tried to disengage her legs and stand but he grabbed her bottom and held firm. Evidently, he wasn't finished with her yet. Without a word, he turned and carried her back toward the house.

"You left the water running," she joked, trying to remind herself this was about fun and nothing else. But her voice came out all strangled.

"It's one of those newfangled systems that turns itself off. I'm more interested in turning things on." His gaze fastened on her breasts and not even the cool rain could stop her body from warming all over.

Too bad not even hot sex could melt the ice around Harrison's heart.

***

Harrison's guts churned. He should never have agreed to this holiday affair. But the chemistry between him and Jade had stunned him with its intensity. His body had bargained with his mind that it would be better to get it out of his system rather than dwell on what could have been. Now, he wasn't so sure. The sex had lived up to its promise. It was the best he'd ever had. Since Emily, he'd restricted himself to plain vanilla, not daring to push the limits and test his self-control. With Jade, that hadn't been an option. If he hadn't taken control, she would have, and he'd have been even more doomed.

His plan had backfired. Stupendously failed. Was he a kid again that he'd do something so stupid as let himself go and forget about birth control? Had he learned nothing? Except the sensation of sliding his bare cock into Jade's hot, slick pussy had been beyond his wildest imagining. And it was something he couldn't wait to do again. And again. God, this woman was an addiction he couldn't control.

An addiction that, in five hours, he'd be saying goodbye to forever. *Over my dead body* floated into his brain. It would probably come to that.

"What does your next week hold?" he asked, trying to get his soul on board for this departure.

"I'm translating in the deportation trial of an Indonesian illegal immigrant," she replied. Her voice was a bit rough, as though she too was struggling with their imminent parting. Or maybe that was just his wishful thinking, and her throat was simply hoarse from screaming his name. She'd wrapped her white cover-up around her body again, but it was still slightly damp, and he could see her nipples jutting against the soft cotton fabric. His mouth watered.

"Do you enjoy that kind of work?"

"Not really. Most of these people have come to the country illegally because they were desperate. They're not criminals. It breaks my heart to hear what they've left behind and risked for a chance at a new start. I find it hard to keep impartial."

"Then why do it?"

Jade shrugged. "It pays the bills."

That wasn't something he had to worry about anymore. He forked more pad thai into his mouth, enjoying the tangy flavors. When Jade came to Vancouver, he'd take her on a culinary tour of the city's eclectic restaurants.

Wait… Jade, coming to Vancouver? Could she? Would she? Of course, he'd have to make it clear that it would just be a continuation of their affair. He'd told her he wouldn't marry again. Would she understand it was just about sex?

Is it?

He shut down the niggling thought with the ruthlessness of a trial lawyer.

If it wasn't for his promise to his father to keep the company running during his health crisis, Harrison would be able to free up his calendar to take a long holiday in Australia.

Dammit, the woman was a distraction. He had to get away before he was living in this shack full time, with no electricity, taking showers in the rain. Although washing outside had its merits ... like seeing Jade's naked body in full daylight, soapy and chilled, her skin alive to his touch.

"And after the trial?" How soon could he invite her to his hometown?

"My friend Karly is getting married and I'm her maid of honor, so I've got lots of wedding stuff to do."

If he asked her about her plans after the wedding, he'd come across as desperate, so he just nodded.

Jade took his empty plate and put it with hers on the coffee table. Then she straddled him on the swinging sofa. After their "shower," she'd convinced him to let her put on an Indonesian sarong. He had to admit, the skirt was less hindrance to his nearly constant erection. If he wasn't inside Jade, it seemed he wanted to be.

"Want to be my plus-one at the wedding?" she asked. Her loosely bound breasts were right in front of his face, begging to be licked, sucked, worshipped.

"When is it?" He was already unwrapping her. After all, he was on the clock.

"Six weeks. I'll send you the details." Her eyes glazed with passion, and her breathing grew rapid and shallow.

"I'll have my secretary put it on my calendar." His lips clamped down on her already hard nipple, and he focused his attention on making sure she never forgot him.

While he pretended this was just about sex.

His phone alarm went off hours later when he was buried deep within her. Having been assured she was on the pill and they were both healthy, he'd forgone condoms, and for the first time since his wife had died, he'd enjoyed sex without a sheath.

"I have to go," he said, forcing his body to leave the heaven of hers. "A car will collect me in twenty minutes and take me to the airport."

"I was going to drive you." She flopped onto her back, not bothering to cover her incredible body. It took everything he had to leave the bed.

"Stay here and rest. I don't like public goodbyes." The thought of them parting at the airport had nearly killed him, so he'd arranged for a car to pick him up. Giving directions had been a nightmare, so he'd just relayed his geographical coordinates. It was anyone's guess whether he'd be picked up or not. Personally, he was hoping for not. He'd take any excuse to spend another day with Jade…

He ran a damp washcloth over his body before pulling on his clothes. If he made it in time, he'd shower in the lounge at the airport. When he returned to the bedroom, Jade had rolled to her side and pulled the sheet up to her waist. Her eyes were closed, but they opened as he sat on the side of the bed.

"Really, I can take you," she said.

"Can you stand?"

She stretched, and the sheet slid away. He stifled a groan. He should've known Jade wouldn't make this easy.

"Good point. My legs don't seem to be working."

He traced the outline of her upper-thigh tattoo with his finger, a satisfied smile curving his lips as she pulled in a shuddery breath. Even after all they'd done, a single touch still affected her. "What does this say?"

"If you can read this, thank a teacher."

"Really?" He traced the intricate script with his tongue. The smell of her sex filled his head and he forgot his question.

"It says, 'Love is an illusion. Only oceans last forever.'"

He lifted his head, his eyes meeting hers. "Is that what you believe?"

She swallowed. "I did at the time."

He was too afraid to ask what had changed her mind. She'd said she wanted a love that could move mountains. His couldn't even stop a spiral into addiction. He'd dumped all his shit at her feet and never asked what had left her so disillusioned about relationships. Reaching into his pocket, he pulled out a flash drive and handed it to her.

"What's this?" She fingered the small device. "You didn't video record our time here, did you?"

"I wish. Then I'd have something interesting to watch on the seventeen-hour flight home."

"So what is it, then?"

She'd sat up, her legs tucked behind her. He closed her hand around the flash drive and put his lips against hers. "It's the twenty-first century version of a mixed tape."

"*Eat Pray Love* had a happy ending," she whispered.

"It was also a movie."

"Did your secretary make this for you?" Her eyes were glassy, as if she was about to cry.

"No, I selected the songs the night we played that game in the bar." The night he couldn't sleep because his thoughts were too full of her. Emotions began to choke him. He had to leave. Now. "Thank you for an amazing week, Jade. Send me the date of your friend's wedding and I'll see if I can get away."

"One kiss before you go?"

She sat up on her knees, her breasts pressing against his arm.

"Witch. If I kiss you, I'll never leave."

"That's what I was hoping." Her lips connected with his and her hands slid up his chest and into his hair.

His groan filled the room, but before she could deepen the embrace, he pulled out of her arms. Damn, this was hard.

"Goodbye, Jade."

He strode from the room before his legs refused to leave. The way his body was defecting, he'd be lucky to make it to the road where his car waited.

Forget fixing—Bali had damn near destroyed him.

Chapter Thirteen

Harrison had been back in Canada for three days now, and every second of it, he wished he was still in Bali. The normal relief he felt at crawling into his own bed was negated by the absence of Jade. And meetings were interminable without her whispering a translation into his ear. If he didn't get her out of his mind soon, he'd go insane.

"Thank you, gentlemen. I'll let you know my decision by the end of the day." It would be no, of course, because he hadn't heard a thing they'd said.

The boardroom door hadn't even closed behind them before his sister pushed it open. "Yo, Harrison, ready to do lunch?" Sonia's exuberance always brought a smile to his face. No wonder she wasn't taken seriously in the business community. She looked like a cheerleader who'd misplaced her pom-poms.

He took in her leggings and her top, which was either a long shirt or a very short dress. Coupled with her ponytail and her flat shoes, she was the antithesis of a corporate executive. "You'd get more respect if you dressed appropriately for the workplace, you know."

She shrugged one shoulder, as if she couldn't be bothered to lift both. "I like to take people by surprise. They think I'm all dumb and sweet, and then *bam!* I slay them with my brain." She did a few karate chops and one high kick into the air to prove her point. "Anyway, you're stuffy enough for both of us."

He wasn't getting into this with her today. Not when he was jetlagged and going through Jade withdrawals.

"I'll be ready for lunch in a couple of minutes. I need to check my messages first." What he needed to do was to stop looking at his phone every five minutes to see if Jade had contacted him. She'd sent him one photo on Sunday—a black-and-white shot of her back while she meditated on her deck with the amazing view in the distance. The only thing she'd had on was a set of headphones. It was captioned, "Listening to a mixed tape." His cock twitched just remembering the picture.

His phone buzzed as he held it in his hand.

Jade: Thank you for the peonies. Six dozen seems excessive, though.

He flopped back into the chair to reply. When they'd exchanged contact information, he'd been pleased she'd given him her home address as well as phone numbers.

Harrison: Not really. I had to stop at six because that's all they had. You definitely redefined pleasure for me.

Jade: I had fun too. How was your flight back? You feeling okay?

Harrison: Fine to both. Had a nine-hour layover in Seoul, so went to visit my grandparents. Realized my Korean language skills suck. Have always relied on my mother to translate. Do you speak Korean?

Jade: No, but I can learn.

She'd learn Korean for him? His stupid heart fibrillated.

Harrison: How's the trial?

Jade: Soul-destroying. Woman was beaten by her husband back in Sumatra but doesn't look like she'll be able to stay in Oz because she's not a political refugee. Was so sick yesterday I could barely stand but managed to survive.

Harrison: That's too bad for the woman. Why were you sick? Are you feeling better now?

Jade: Some kind of stomach bug. Got sick soon after you left. Just managed to make my plane on Sunday. Spent the whole previous night throwing up. Glad to hear you're okay. Would hate your last memory of Bali to be bad.

His last memory of Bali had been Jade naked on the bed, asking him to stay. He still wasn't sure why he was back in Vancouver.

Harrison: Look after yourself.

He hesitated, his fingers on the keyboard, desperate to ask the question he didn't want to know the answer to. Did she miss him?

Jade: What are you wearing?

It was minefield territory for his sanity, but he rushed right in.

Harrison: Charcoal suit, black shoes and belt, white shirt, burgundy tie. And you?

The last two words were courtesy of his cock.

Jade: Nothing. Still in bed. Have to get up in ten minutes and get ready for work. Just wanting to check you were okay first.

He closed his eyes on the mental image, and the phone fell from his hands onto the table. It buzzed again and he snatched it up.

Jade: I'm imagining your burgundy tie wrapped around my wrists, anchoring me to the bed while you pound into me from behind. Guess it's shower time now. Enjoy the rest of your Monday. Jade out.

A loud groan filled the air.

"What's wrong with you?"

Shit. He'd forgotten his sister was still in the room.

He leapt to his feet. "Nothing. Ready for lunch?"

"Nice try, big brother. Who were you texting?"

Sonia grabbed for his phone, but considering she was almost a foot shorter than him, he was easily able to hold it out of her reach.

"No one who concerns you."

"Oh my God, you've got a girlfriend. Wait until Mom hears."

She picked up her own phone and was about to ring their mother when he snatched it out of her hand.

"I said, it doesn't concern you."

An evil smile transformed his sister's face from that of a bubbly cheerleader to a lethal assassin. Had he underestimated her like all the others? She strode out the door and around the corner. By the time he caught up with her, she was grilling his secretary about his recent business trip.

"He did ask me to organize a romantic dinner," Lisa—his long-time but about-to-be fired personal assistant—divulged. "He said expense was not to be considered and to make it a night to remember."

Sonia bounced up and down and clapped. "Yes! You met someone. A local? Or a woman on holiday?"

He closed his eyes and the groan that escaped his throat this time had nothing to do with missed pleasure or erotic images. His sister was as tenacious as a dog with its favorite chew toy. His only hope was to give her the barest of details and pray that would suffice.

"All right. I met someone. But she lives in Australia and I live in Canada, so nothing can come of it. End of story."

Sonia glared at him and put one hand on her hip. "You may not have heard, what with your head up your ass most of the time, but they've made these amazing things called planes. Now you can go to Australia without having to spend six months on a boat."

"I'm well aware of the benefits of international travel. But I'm not interested in a long-distance relationship." Sonia's eyes lit up so he quickly added, "Or any relationship, for that matter. It was fun while we were together but we both went into the affair knowing it was temporary."

"And yet here you are, still texting her." Her eyes went wide. "You moaned. You were sexting! Stop the presses! My staid-as-an-old-maid brother was sexting with a woman he met in a foreign country!"

If she yelled it any louder, Jade would be able to hear her over in Australia. He let the *staid* comment pass. Jade would refute that claim based on the number of times and ways he'd brought her to climax. Heat crept up his neck to his face, making him look even guiltier. If he was at a trial, and the defendant reacted this way, he'd go for the jugular. Based on the gleam in his sister's eyes, she'd spotted his weakness and was about to launch her attack. Why the hell had he ever thought her young and naïve?

"She was sick and messaged me to make sure I was okay. The moan was…"

"Do you have a picture of her?" She grabbed for his phone, and catching him by surprise, managed to pry it from his hand.

"Sonia, don't." He put as much menace as possible into his tone, but it didn't even slow his sister down. Unfortunately, the phone was still on the message screen, and it only took a second for her to find the photo of Jade on the deck.

"Holy shit, bro. What the hell are you doing here? Do you have any pictures of her face? Or were you only interested in her body?"

He was not discussing Jade's figure with his little sister. Or all the other things about Jade that he found so fascinating.

"Enough." He grabbed the phone from his sister's hands and thrust it in his pocket. It pressed against his erection that had sprung to life at the mention of his time with Jade, and he just managed to suppress another moan.

"One last question," Sonia said.

"We're done here. And I've lost my appetite. Get your own lunch." He moved toward his office but Sonia's voice stopped him at the door.

"Give me her name, or I'll tell Mom and she'll get the information out of you. Although I'm not sure if she'll approve of that photo."

He banged his forehead twice on his closed office door, praying he'd wake up from this nightmare and be back in Jade's bed. Or better yet, showering in the rain. "Jade," he replied without turning.

"Jade what?"

He didn't need to turn to know Sonia was already doing a Google search on her phone.

"Irvine. Jade Irvine, and she was my translator."

"Fabulous. You can tell me the rest over lunch." Sonia grabbed his arm and pulled him toward the elevator.

"There is no 'rest.' This conversation is finished."

Sonia laughed. Life, as he knew it, was over.

***

Jade stirred her drink with the swizzle stick and pretended to listen to her friends' conversation, which mostly centered around the wedding on the weekend. As the maid of honor, she should be contributing, but she was concentrating too much on keeping her lunch down to do more than nod. The bar wasn't busy on a Monday mid-afternoon, so they'd had their pick of seats. The corner booth, right under the air conditioning and photos of Kakadu, was currently Wedding Central Station.

"You still moping about that man you left behind in Bali?" Karly asked. "For God's sake, Jade, it's been six weeks. I haven't seen you like this over a guy since the shithead-who-shall-not-be-named screwed you over."

Jade forced a smile. *I think I'm pregnant, but I'm too chicken to find out for sure*, she wanted to blurt out. Instead she replied, "I'm not moping. I'm just not feeling great. I promise I'll be in top form for the wedding."

"You decided yet whether you're bringing a date? I need to firm up the seating chart and laminate it before Hugh's mother makes one more suggestion about moving her family closer to the head table." Once Karly laminated something, there was no changing it … as her future mother-in-law was about to find out.

A waitress walked by with a bowl of beef stew and Jade turned her head until the nausea passed. "I'll let you know by tomorrow. I invited him, but he hasn't confirmed. His dad is having some sort of artery unblocking procedure today, and Harrison wants to make sure that goes well before he books anything."

They'd been texting back and forth almost daily since she'd returned to Australia. She'd tried to stop, tried to put him out of her mind and concentrate on her life and her best friend's wedding. But as soon as something interesting happened, Harrison was the one she wanted to tell. If she was bored or down, he was the one she texted to bring a smile to her face.

Last week had been the worst. As the nausea had become daily and undeniable, she'd sent him a photo of her naked breasts captioned, "Your friends are missing you."

He'd replied with, "You. Are. Killing. Me."

Which she assumed was a good thing. Fortunately or not, no dick picture had followed. But he'd replied to her next message, so she figured he wasn't too put off by her.

If he did come for the wedding, she'd have to tell him about the potential baby. In fact, she'd have to know for sure before he came. If he didn't show, she could go on for a little longer in a state of denial. Until her belly button popped out and she could no longer fasten her jeans.

"Earth to Jade."

"Sorry. Zoned out again." She met the worried faces of her friends.

Karly put her hand over Jade's on the table, the three-carat diamond almost blinding her. "Is this too hard for you, sweetie? I thought you were over asshole-with-a-wife. If I'd known my wedding was going to upset you, I'd never have said yes to Hugh."

Jade laughed. "I'm over him. Long ago." She attempted a pre-Bali Jade comment, something she might have said before she'd met Harrison. "Just trying to work out which of the groomsmen I'm going to drop my dress for."

"As long as it's not my Cooper," Jules said,

twirling her own engagement ring. The latest of their foursome to give up her freedom, Jules was almost unbearably happy. Jade's heart twanged with jealousy.

"He's all yours," Jade said, then made a gagging face to her other friends. While they laughed, she checked her phone for a message from Harrison.

If she was pregnant, she'd have to tell her baby daddy. It was not a conversation she was looking forward to. Given his past, she knew it was the last thing he'd want to hear from her. But not telling him wasn't an option. If he found out by accident, he'd be devastated. Harrison Mackenzie was a man who took his responsibilities very seriously. What if he insisted on sole custody? He was rich, with a loving family— a judge would consider it.

She took a sip of her fizzy water, hoping to quell the urge to hurl. At first, she'd thought it was just a recurrence of the virus that had leveled her back in Indonesia. She hadn't been able to keep anything down for two days. Including her contraceptive pills. But since eating a little and drinking fizzy water helped ease her queasiness, she knew this was different. Add in her tender breasts, near-constant state of exhaustion, and a month-late period, and the signs were becoming hard to ignore. Of course, her periods were often irregular, so maybe she was worrying for nothing.

Jules reached over and grabbed Jade's drink, giving it a suspicious sniff. "Are you drinking club soda? You must be sick." Lauren put the back of her hand on Jade's forehead.

"I'm fine. I'm saving up for the wedding. Nothing says classy country club nuptials quite like a shit-faced maid of honor shagging the third groomsman under the cake table."

The girls all laughed, and Jade was able to let the wedding talk flow around her again. Karly's fiancé, Hugh, came from old money, and their wedding was to be the society event of the year, with upward of five hundred guests. If Hugh wasn't such a great guy, Jade would be having a serious talk with her friend about marrying into that mafia. But the man doted on Karly, and Jade had never seen her friend so happy. So Jade would smile and give a funny toast and forget that after Harrison, any man she chose to wed would be a step down. He'd said he'd never marry again, and given the sternness of his expression, she believed him.

"Have you decided what to take on honeymoon yet?" Jade asked, knowing this would steer the conversation away from her and take at least half an hour for Karly to answer. She'd spent more time worrying about her trousseau than the actual ceremony, although Karly's mother-in-law-to-be had pretty much insisted on having her way for most of those decisions.

A cleared throat brought her attention back to the group. "And the last thing on today's agenda"—Karly stopped for a dramatic pause, and all eyes turned to Jade—"is the rota."

"Rota?" she asked. Had they discussed this before? Aside from today, she'd been fully involved in the wedding planning. Well, the part that Karly had done anyway.

"Who is going to take the first shift in monitoring Jade?"

"What? Why do I need monitoring?"

Again, all eyes turned to her. Karly put her hand on Jade's again. "Sweetie, you have a tendency to … find trouble."

"I—"

"It's one of the things we love about you the most," Jules interjected. "There's rarely a dull moment when you're around. But this is Karly's big day, and it has to go off without a hitch or she'll never hear the end of it from Hugh's mum."

Little did they know that trouble had likely already found Jade. If only the affair had stayed in Bali and not latched onto her uterus. Her hand strayed to her still-flat belly. Did a little life grow inside her? A part of Harrison to keep forever?

"I promise to be on my best behavior." Unfortunately, the vow wasn't enough to satisfy her friends. Geez, tough crowd. "And my dad is coming to the wedding and reception. I can guarantee that he'll keep an eagle eye on me." That did the trick, and the conversation turned to the order in which they would get their hair done, allowing Jade to zone out again.

"Jade, can you come with me for a sec?" She looked up to find Karly standing next to her, a determined look on her face.

"You want me to practice holding your dress while you pee?" She dutifully followed her friend into the ladies' room at the back of the bar.

Karly peered under all the stalls and seemed satisfied the room was empty except for them. Was she going to tell her she'd changed her mind about the wedding and wanted Jade to help her break the news to Hugh? No. Her eyes still held that stupid-in-love glow they'd had since the day Karly had first laid eyes on her husband-to-be.

Karly leaned against one of the sinks and crossed her arms over her chest. "How long have we been friends?"

Maybe Karly was going to tell her she'd been fired as maid of honor. Jade knew the future monster-in-law hadn't been happy with Karly's choice. The Irvines did not run in the same circles as Hugh's family.

"Fifteen years, give or take a few months when you didn't speak to me because Bobby Driscoll kissed me and not you at the surf competition." A flicker of amusement crossed Karly's eyes before she became serious again.

"So don't you think, after fifteen years of being best friends, I would know when something is bothering you?"

Busted. "Um, yeah, I guess."

"I'm going to ask you a question, Jade. And if you want our friendship—which I treasure more than my diamond ring, and that's pretty stupendous—to last one more day, then you will give me an honest answer."

Jade swallowed down a rise in nausea. Now was not the time to lose her chips all over her best friend's

Jimmy Choos. "I swear on our friendship to tell you the truth." It was a vow they'd made to each other several times over the course of their history, and neither had broken it once.

"Is Hugh cheating on me? Is that what's got you so upset? Did you catch him with another woman and you don't know how to tell me, five days before the wedding?"

"No!" Jade wrapped an arm around her friend, whose knees had given way with relief. "Hugh loves you and only you. And, for the record, if I'd have caught him cheating, I'd have presented his nuts to you on one of his mother's silver plates."

"Thank God. I didn't think it possible, but you seemed so worried."

"It's not that. So no need to fret." Jade hugged her friend again and started toward the door only to have her arm wrenched back.

"What is it, then? And don't you dare try to pretend it's nothing. You're drinking fizzy water on half-price margarita day, and I know you don't have to work tomorrow, because you took the week off for me."

"I… I'll tell you after the wedding."

"No way, sister. Here and now."

Jade stared into her best friend's eyes. "I might be pregnant."

Chapter Fourteen

A tremor of excitement rippled through Harrison as he ascended the steps to the country club. Attending some strangers' wedding was not on his list of favorite things to do. But seeing Jade was. He shouldn't be this excited to see a woman he'd spent less than a week with. But he was. Despite his sister's constant harassment over the past seven weeks, he was still adamant this was just a fling. The second he thought maybe he was ready for more, the memory of finding Emily's lifeless body lying on the kitchen floor would come back to haunt him.

A long weekend of sex, however, was definitely on the menu. Weddings were a woman's aphrodisiac. That was one of the reasons he was here. He wasn't ready to be replaced just yet.

His flight had been delayed, so he'd missed the ceremony, but Jade had told him not to worry. Her maid-of-honor duties would keep her too busy to spend any time with him until after dinner. The reception had been scheduled to start half an hour before, but if he knew anything about society weddings, the receiving line would barely have moved.

Despite his family's current wealth, his father's blue-collar background had grounded them, and the only membership the Mackenzies held was to Costco. But he'd been to enough weddings of business associates to know how these dog-and-pony shows went. It was less about the bride and groom and more about the parents displaying their wealth and status.

A woman in a business dress checked his name off the list, and he stepped into the ballroom, his eyes searching for Jade. It took only a second for him to find her, since she stood next to the bride, her body swathed in an emerald-green silk dress that he knew would show off her amazing eyes. However, as he'd predicted, the line to congratulate the newlywed couple was at least fifty people long. A passing waiter handed him a glass of champagne, and he joined the lineup.

"Hello, young man. You weren't at the wedding. I would have remembered you." The elderly lady in front of him turned around and looked him over as if he were a slab of chocolate cake and she'd just come off a diet.

"I flew in from Canada and missed the ceremony. I'm a guest of Jade Irvine, the maid of honor."

The octogenarian ran an arthritic finger over the lapel of his jacket. "I'm Celia, the bride's grandmother. I've known Jade since she was a little girl."

"Pleased to meet you, Celia. I'm Harrison. Do you have any stories you could tell me about Jade?"

"What's it worth to you?"

He didn't trust the gleam in the old lady's eyes. "What kind of currency are we talking?"

"First dance."

"Sold."

The bargaining done, she kept him entertained for the next twenty minutes, telling him about all the times Jade had lured her granddaughter, Karly, into trouble.

"And those four girls caught every single koi from the water feature in front of their school and carried them to the lake a kilometer away so the fish could have more room to swim. Of course, any that managed to survive the trek were probably eaten within minutes by the larger creatures already calling the lake home."

Celia clung to his arm, her eyes alive with laughter. Every few minutes, she'd emphasize a point by running a hand down his chest. Please God, he hoped the first dance wasn't a slow number.

"Sounds like Jade was a bad influence on your granddaughter and her other friends." Maybe it was just the grandmother's bias, but every story had featured Jade as the instigator in the adventure.

"Jade was Karly's savior. Without her, Karly would have ended up like all the other brittle women in this room, who think their worth is measured by the size of their husband's bank account. The Feisty Four, as they call themselves, are women to be reckoned with. I couldn't be prouder of the lot of them."

A strange squiggly feeling invaded Harrison's chest.

They finally reached the bridal party. Celia introduced him as if he were her date, and not a single person batted an eyelash. He shook hands and made inane comments about how beautiful the room was, or impressive the building, impatient for the moment when he'd stand in front of the woman who'd been constantly in his thoughts for the past seven weeks.

There was a clog in the line as someone monopolized the groom's time. Near enough now to see her in full, Harrison stared at Jade. All the waiting had not prepared him for her beauty. The floor-length green dress hugged her form and emphasized her curves. The deep valley between her breasts called for his tongue to explore its hidden treasures. Her black hair had been styled with such intricacy, interwoven with red rose buds and tiny white flowers, that it would take hours to release the strands for his fingers to slide through.

"Look who I found, Jade, dear," Celia said. "He says he's your date, but I'll keep him entertained until you're free."

"Thank you, Granny Celia," Jade said. "I knew I could count on you to find the handsomest single man here and lay claim to him."

Celia finally moved on to greet her granddaughter, and Harrison was in front of Jade.

"You look spectacular," he whispered into her ear. His lips grazed her cheek, and he lingered longer than politeness dictated, but he didn't care. He inhaled her lemony-ginger scent. The heat from her body released the vice grip around his chest that had prevented him from taking a full breath since he'd walked out her door in Bali.

"You wore your kilt."

Her gaze swept up from his brogues and hose,

lingered a long moment on the sporran hiding his growing erection, then slid up his white shirt and black waistcoat and jacket to his bow tie. When her gaze met his, there was no denying the passion arcing between them.

Then a flicker of what he could only describe as fear flashed through her emerald eyes, and he took a step back.

"Are you okay?"

She pulled herself together, wiping a hand down her dress. "Better than fine, now that you're here." She leaned toward him and brushed her lips against his. "I can't tell you how happy I am to see you again."

Before he could reply, she'd turned to the next guest in the line, her thumb and middle finger fused together.

***

"I cannot believe I've been upstaged at my own wedding. And by a man." Karly's gaze followed Harrison around the floor. "Do you think he's wearing anything under that kilt?"

That same thought had been on constant replay in Jade's brain since she'd spotted him joining the back of the queue for the receiving line next to Granny Celia. Her pseudo-grandmother hadn't let go of Harrison. Not that Jade could blame her.

"He does look good," Jade agreed. Better than good. Lingerie-melting fantastic. More important, the butterflies she'd experienced their whole time together in Bali had reappeared, fluttering throughout her abdomen and chest. She'd convinced herself that she'd imagined the connection—that in her mind, the long absence had distorted how she felt when she was near him. No such luck. Harrison affected her in a way no other man ever had. And, she feared, never would again.

Karly's exaggerated sigh brought Jade's attention back to her. "My marriage isn't valid until it's consummated, is it?"

If it had been any woman other than her best friend looking at Harrison like that, Jade would've had her flat on the floor with a roundhouse kick by now. As it was, Granny Celia was treading a thin line.

"You pre-consummated your marriage, remember?" Jade dropped her gaze pointedly to her friend's waist. When she'd confessed her pregnancy fears to Karly on Monday, her friend had whipped a couple test kits out of her bag, saying she'd had the same problems. They'd sat in stalls side by side and both discovered they were mothers-to-be.

"You two are going to have the most gorgeous baby. If it's prettier than mine, I may never speak to you again."

"Shush," Jade said. "I haven't told him yet."

"Well, if I were you, I'd wait until after you discover if he's free-balling it under that kilt."

There was no right moment for that conversation. She'd just have to play it by ear. But yeah, naked might be the best option.

Jade clinked glasses of ginger ale with her friend

as Hugh came to claim his bride.

"They're going to announce us now," he said. "Mrs. Karly Peters. I will never get tired of hearing that."

Pure love and amazement shone from the big man's eyes, and a twinge pinched Jade's heart. Hugh had been delighted to find out he and Karly were going to be parents. Jade had no hope that Harrison would react the same way.

She filed into position with the rest of the wedding party behind the bride and groom. The head table was up on a dais, giving her a great view of the room. Karly had shown Jade the seating plan and asked her where to put Harrison as soon as he'd confirmed that he was coming, and so Jade knew where he'd be. Table twelve, with several of Hugh's rugby buddies and two couples Jade knew to be fun. Somehow, Granny Celia had switched the name cards and now sat next to Harrison. Jade glanced at table six, where Celia should have been, to find the scrum-half from Hugh's rugby team sitting among a selection of elderly relatives, a puzzled expression on his face.

A laugh erupted from Jade's throat and Karly looked over. "Granny Celia's up to her old tricks," Jade said, gesturing with a nod of her head at the change in tables.

"I want to be just like her when I get old," Karly replied. "Although hopefully, I'll just have the one husband."

"I heard her two husbands both died of exhaustion," Hugh said. "Not a bad way to go, if you ask me."

"I've already tested your stamina. You'll do fine, sunshine."

Again, Jade had to look away from the love on display before a tear escaped.

The meal dragged on, especially since Jade could barely eat. The anticipation of being with Harrison again, coupled with the news she had to give him, had her guts churning. Or was that morning sickness? As one uneaten course was replaced by the next, she often heard Harrison's deep chuckle over the general buzz of conversation. Her eyes kept drifting to his table, which seemed to be the liveliest one in the whole room. The dessert course was accompanied by the speeches and toasts, which were excruciating, including her own maid-of-honor homage to the bride. She'd stumbled over her words, tears rendering her written notes unreadable. Finally, Karly had shut her up with a fierce hug and whispered, "blame the pregnancy hormones," in her ear.

Her maid-of-honor duties over at last, Jade could circulate with the rest of the guests. She'd barely stepped off the dais when Harrison was at her side.

"If you've come to tell me you're throwing me over for Celia, I understand," Jade said when he just stared at her.

"Where can we go that's private?"

She searched his eyes. He couldn't know, could he? A flicker of fear clutched her heart. "Is something wrong?" Her heart was in her throat as she asked the question. He wouldn't fly halfway around the world to tell her to stop texting him, that there was someone else in his life, would he?

"I need to kiss you. Now."

She nodded, grabbed his hand, and exited the ballroom. A few doors down, a security guard sat outside a closed door. He recognized her and opened it. She ushered Harrison inside and then locked the door behind them. All the bridal party's handbags and stuff were in there, as well as the outfit Karly was going to change into later in the evening.

"I have to be back in five minutes for the bridal party dance," she said, a bit breathless.

Harrison's lips were already on hers before she'd even finished the sentence. He tasted like coffee and chocolate cake and kissed her until the room spun.

"I've missed you," he said, his voice husky. "I've booked a suite at The Langham. The second you say the word, we're out of here … although I do understand this is your friend's wedding and you may want to stay until the end." He gave her a sexy grin that flicked every lust switch she had to the "on" position.

She ran her hands down his buttocks, searching for a hint of underwear. After all, a girl needed to know what she was dealing with. "I thought we'd just go to my place."

His lips were doing wicked things to her ear. "Last time you took me to your place, it had no running water or electricity. I'm not risking that again."

"I thought you liked the rain shower."

"That's a Bali exclusive."

His lips recaptured hers just as there was a pounding on the door.

"Jade, I know you're in there." Lauren's laugh-filled voice infiltrated the lust haze Harrison had evoked. "Karly sent me to get you; the dancing is about to start."

"Seems this will have to wait," Harrison said, stepping away.

"Before we go…" She put a hand out and touched his sporran. How could a man make a skirt look so damned sexy and masculine? "Just how Scottish are you?"

"As Scottish as the heather that kisses the feet of Ben Nevis," he replied in a deep Scottish brogue.

A shiver ran up her spine, spun her brain like a whirligig, then raced back down to settle in her ovaries, where it burst into heat. *Hot. Damn.* "Remember that accent later."

The pounding on the door resumed, and Jade wrenched it open to see Lauren's smiling face. Her friend's eyes darted straight past Jade to settle on Harrison. "If you need someone to keep him company for a while…"

"Hands off, Loly. He's mine." Even though he wasn't really. She could lay no claim to Harrison, except perhaps as the mother of his child. The heat in her belly withered, and the shiver that wracked her this time was ice-cold trepidation.

Harrison gave her an odd look but wrapped an arm around her waist and escorted her back to the ballroom. Karly and Hugh were already on the dance floor, swaying to "All of Me" by John Legend. Jade quickly wiped away the tear that had formed in the corner of her eye. Karly was right: pregnancy hormones were a bitch.

"I promised the first dance to Celia in exchange for stories of your childhood," Harrison whispered into her ear. His warm breath slid down the v of her dress to nestle between her breasts. "But after that, I'm claiming every dance with you."

"She told you about the koi, didn't she?"

"Yup. Among other things." His mischievous smile did wicked things to her lady parts.

The song came to an end, the audience clapped for the bride and groom, and then Stuart, the best man, came and claimed her for the bridal party dance. "Damn, I thought I might have a chance with you tonight," he said as he whirled her around the floor.

She glanced over at Harrison. He stood front and center, his arms crossed over his broad chest, his eyes never leaving her. Stuart was tall, good-looking in a metrosexual kind of way, and quite charming. Before Harrison, he might have been her under-the-cake-table partner. But now, not a chance.

"Sorry. I'm spoken for." At least for tonight. Possibly for the rest of her on-earth existence.

The song changed, and the floor opened up to family and close friends. Jade found herself in her dad's arms while a gleeful Celia clung to Harrison.

"Who's the bloke what can't take his eyes off you?"

"Harrison Mackenzie. I met him a couple months back in Bali. I invited him." If she thought that was going to appease her father, she was sadly mistaken.

"What kind of man wears a skirt?"

"A sexy one" probably wasn't the answer he was looking for. "It's a kilt. His father's from Scotland. Harrison lives in Canada."

"He's come a long way for a date. Bring him round for lunch tomorrow."

Her dad kept his arm firmly around her shoulders when the dance ended, so she had to introduce him to Harrison. Aside from a small smile when they shook hands, she couldn't tell if her father approved or not. Not that it really mattered—their lives were all about to become inexorably linked. God, she'd have to tell her dad at some point, too. Hopefully around her third trimester.

"Your father reminds me of mine," Harrison said as he twirled her around the dance floor. He was light on his feet for a big man. "When my sister was eighteen, some guy took an interest in her. My dad wore the same expression yours does. He thinks I'm up to no good."

"Aren't you?" She leaned back in his arms so she could see his face.

Harrison smiled down at her. "No. I'm very, very good."

She couldn't argue with that. She nestled her cheek against his chest and just enjoyed being held in his arms.

The rest of the wedding was like a Disney fantasy.

If they weren't dancing, then Harrison kept his arm around her waist and chatted with her friends or stole kisses from her on the terrace. When it came time for the cake cutting, Karly first lifted the tablecloth to check underneath. Jade, Jules, and Lauren all burst into laughter. Harrison looked puzzled.

"I'll explain later," she said.

"I doubt you'll have the breath to talk later, but okay."

Tomorrow. She was definitely going to tell him about the baby tomorrow.

Tonight was all for her.

Chapter Fifteen

It was two in the morning before the taxi dropped them at The Langham. They'd stayed at the reception until the end and then had one last drink with the rest of the bridal party—minus Karly and Hugh, who were off to consummate their marriage … probably in the back of the limo on the way to their hotel, if Jade was to hazard a guess.

She sensed Harrison's impatience to get her alone, but she was delaying the time when she'd have to tell him about the baby. She was living the fantasy that they were in love and dreaming of their own wedding. There was no need to harsh her mellow with life's fetal realities.

"I'm going to have to do the walk of shame again tomorrow," she said as they rode the lift to his floor. And there'd be no helicopter this time to ease the sting.

"I've got tomorrow's wardrobe covered. My sister sent a dress for you. I was damn glad my bags weren't searched in customs."

Wait. What? "Your sister sent clothes for me to wear after a night of hot sex?"

He laughed. "She didn't put it quite like that. She said she wanted to send something for you and I agreed, as long as I got to inspect it first. She has good taste. She must have got that from her big brother."

"How'd your sister find out about me—us?" She searched his face. She'd reckoned Harrison wouldn't have told anyone about their time in Bali. He'd never called her from the office, only a few times late at night when he'd been home and couldn't sleep. Not that she'd helped much with his insomnia.

"She caught me texting you and has been blackmailing me for information ever since." He said it nonchalantly, as if extortion was a common occurrence in his family. As an only child, Jade had never had that sort of relationship. The closest thing she had to siblings were Karly, Jules, and Lauren.

Jade scowled. "Blackmailing you? How?"

"By threatening to tell my mother."

A yawning chasm opened inside her. "You don't want your mother to find out about me?"

He kissed her lightly on the lips, then the lift doors slid open and he ushered her out and down the corridor. "It has nothing to do with being embarrassed about being with you. I'm protecting you from a stalker. You do not want my mother on your back. She would be calling you every day to see how you are, and asking if you're still in love with me."

Wait till she finds out she's going to be a grandmother.

"Who said I'm in love with you at all?"

He slid his card key into the slot, then opened the door. He had a corner suite, the carpet so plush she couldn't wait to sink her aching toes into it. The decor was stunning. But not as gorgeous as the man in the kilt standing in the middle of the floor.

Harrison shrugged. "My mother will assume we're in love."

"Whereas we both know this is just about sex."

He strode over to her and took her jaw in his large hand, his thumb tracing the outline of her bottom lip before his head dipped down to hers. "Is it? I'm not so sure anymore."

His mouth made love to hers. Or maybe she was still delusional from all the amorous looks and comments between Karly and Hugh. But still, there seemed something different about Harrison and the way he touched her. While his lips sipped and caressed hers, his hands flitted over her curves as if he was afraid she'd disappear if he pressed her too hard.

Meanwhile, she slipped a finger under the waistband of his kilt until she was sure he was bare-arsed. "You are naughty," she said as his lips left hers to trail a wake of devastation along her jaw, down her neck to her collarbone. "Have I mentioned how much I love your kilt?" Even though the damn sporran prevented her from touching the real goods. "Karly complained that you looked better than she did."

"No way. The bride and bridesmaids were all stunning, although I did have one particular favorite. Half the men in the room wished they were in kilts whenever you ladies sauntered past."

He discovered the hidden zipper in the side of her dress and slid it down. The exposed skin became a playground for his fingers.

She sucked in a deep breath while she could still remember to breathe. "Why's that?"

"Because the wool and heavy sporran help keep boners under control. There was a lot of wood in that room tonight, and not all of it on the paneling."

"Oh, really? The kilt makes you immune, does it?" Jade pulled out of his arms, took a step back, and slipped off the dress to reveal her lace lingerie.

The heat in his gaze scorched her exposed skin. "Nothing could make me immune to you. Damn, I could stare at you forever."

"You're just going to look?"

"I didn't fly thirteen thousand kilometers to see the sights. Stand over by the window and look out."

Commanding Harrison was back. Gooseflesh broke out on her arms, and her nipples hardened under the flimsy lace. "You're going to take me with all of Melbourne watching?"

"Your pleasure is for my eyes only. As long as the lights are low in here, no one can see in." He moved to stand right behind her, the warmth from his body and the sultry scent of his cologne filling the space. Filling her. "Keep your eyes open, Jade, and watch your world spin out of control."

Her hair was still up from the wedding, and he licked his way from under her ear to the back of her neck. It was the only place he touched her and she ached for his hands on her.

"Harrison…" His name ended on a moan as his tongue traced the outline of her other ear. Still, he kept his body away, knowing it was driving her insane. How could the man make her so wet without even caressing her?

"What happened to 'Harri?'"

"Harri … please."

He got as close as he could without actually making contact. Every nerve, every hair was on high alert. Waiting.

"Please what?"

"For God's sake, just touch me already."

"Is that what you're waiting for? You should have said something earlier. Where do you want me to touch you, Jade? Here on your elbow?"

His thumb swirled circles on her elbow and she almost came right there. If this was what pregnancy did for sex, then she might stay pregnant for the rest of her life. Except for the nausea. That blew chunks. Literally.

"Or maybe here, on your belly button." The index finger of his other hand circled that indentation.

Her breathing was shallow and rapid, and she put both hands on the pane of glass to keep upright. Based on her sweaty palms, the housekeeper was going to need extra-strength cleaner to get her handprints off.

"Maybe you could move your left hand about ten centimeters lower," she suggested.

"Was that lower?" He slipped his finger into the lace waistband of her undies, teasing her curls. "Or higher?" His finger retreated and circled one nipple and then the other through the lace of her bra.

"Harri, I don't give a damn where you touch me. But if you don't soon do something, I'm going to find one of those other men from the wedding with the uncontrollable hard-ons and make their every fantasy come true."

A fierce growl reverberated against her back. "You'll need another man when I'm dead."

Did he realize what he'd said? But before she could analyze his words, the sensual onslaught commenced. His fingers, his lips, hell, even his early-morning stubble made love to her. He loosened her bra but refused to let her drop her arms so it could slide to the floor. Her underpants were wedged halfway down her thighs.

Even after she shouted his name in climax, he continued to caress her, letting her drift slowly back to earth.

She turned, ready to see to his needs, and was shocked at the expression on his face. Maybe he had been serious about a permanent relationship between them. Her heart lightened, and even her nausea took a step back.

"Did you bring your burgundy tie? The one you were going to fasten me to the bed with?" The first thing she and Karly had done upon discovering they were pregnant was to check if sex was still okay. Their combined relief had made them both laugh.

"I'm not going to tie you up. This time. I'm going to kiss and caress every inch of your body until the past seven weeks are a distant nightmare."

Launching orgasm counter.

***

Harrison rolled over to search for the remote to close

the blinds in the bedroom. Why had he forgotten to shut them last night? Oh yeah, because he'd been too busy making Jade shout his name as he brought her from one peak of sexual gratification to the next. They'd both covered a Himalayan mountain range of pleasure last night. He flung his arm over his eyes to block out the light, while his mind caught up with his current situation.

The shower was running in the adjoining bathroom, accounting for Jade's location. And based on the tenting of the sheet covering his lower half, that was where his body wanted to be as well. As soon as he could move.

What wasn't so clear was the next step for their relationship. Because he'd finally admitted to himself that they had one. The constant longing just to hear Jade's voice had been undeniable.

How they could make this work, though, he still hadn't figured out. They could continue the long-distance thing, meeting up for special holidays or occasions and possibly plan a vacation together maybe somewhere halfway, like Hawaii. He couldn't leave Canada. Not only did he have his own venture capital partnership to keep tabs on, but he was running his father's company. Could he ask Jade to uproot herself and move to Canada? Away from her friends, with whom she was obviously very close, and her family? And for what? A let's-see-if-this-can-work scenario? Because the thought of marriage still filled him with dread.

Lying in bed thinking wasn't going to get him

anywhere, so he flung back the sheet and headed to the bathroom.

The shower was running, but Jade sat on the edge of the bathtub, looking very green. She white-knuckled the tile edge with her eyes firmly closed.

"Are you okay?" He raced to her and put a hand on her forehead. She was a bit clammy but didn't seem to be running a fever.

"I'm fine. I must have drunk too much last night."

He took a step back. "You didn't drink anything alcoholic last night. You were on ginger ale and sparkling water. What's going on, Jade? Are you still battling that bug you picked up in Bali?"

Her wan smile held none of the sparkle he'd come to expect from her.

"Bali definitely has something to do with it. Let me have a shower and I'll explain after."

She stood but wobbled and he gathered her into his arms. "I'm calling a doctor."

"No. I have an appointment for Monday."

She already had an appointment scheduled? Was it something serious? His heart stalled, but he forced himself to remain calm. "Okay, but you're spending the rest of the day in bed. You can shower later if you feel better." He started toward the door, but she put on the brakes. Damn stubborn woman, didn't she know he was trying to take care of her? "Back to bed, babe. To sleep. I'm not going to take advantage of a sick woman."

She pulled out of his arms completely. "I don't need to sleep. And my dad is expecting us for lunch at one o'clock."

There it was again, that hint of fear in her eyes. He glanced down at her hand. Yup, thumb and middle finger were joined like they'd been superglued together.

"Are you worried your dad won't like me?" He'd never had to seek parental permission to date a woman before, but he was confident he could handle the challenge. Unless her father asked about his intentions, and if marriage was on the horizon.

"No. Not really."

"Then what? I've seen worry flash in your eyes a few times now. Are you seriously ill?" An icy finger stroked his spine. He couldn't lose Jade. Not now. Not after he'd finally started to move on.

"Let me shower, and then we'll talk. Do you have that outfit your sister sent?"

Before he could protest, she stepped into the shower and he went to get the package from Sonia. When he reentered the bathroom, Jade stood under the shower head, her face upturned while she lathered shampoo through her hair. The erotic image had him instantly hard. But until he knew what was going on with her, sex was off the agenda. If he let her, she'd get his brain lust-fogged and he'd never get a straight answer from her.

Instead, he ordered breakfast and waited for her to emerge from the bathroom. It took almost twenty minutes, but the wait was worth it. She'd braided her damp hair, leaving a few tendrils loose to caress her cheeks, her face was scrubbed clean and makeup-free, and the simple dress she wore set his world on fire. Of course, since her underwear was still on the floor by the sofa where it had ended up last night, he knew she was naked underneath.

She stood hesitantly at the entrance to the sitting room, her fingers playing with the fabric of the dress. "Please thank your sister for me. This outfit is beautiful and super comfy. Or you can give me her number and I can thank her myself."

The silk dress fell in pleats from the scooped neckline, was white at the hem, which sat a couple inches north of her knees, then ranged in shades of blue until it was a navy at the top. Jade looked amazing.

His tongue seemed to have stopped working, so he motioned her over to the table where he'd set up breakfast. She got within two feet and stopped, her fist over her mouth, the color draining from her face as he watched.

"Jade?"

"Could you make me a cup of tea, just milk? And if there's some plain toast, I'll have that over here by the balcony."

He made her requested plate and brought it over to her. An uneasy itch tickled his skin. Then the blood drained from his own face. She couldn't be…

"Sit down, Harri. I can't think when you loom over me."

He took the chair across from her, his stomach too knotted to bother with breakfast now.

"I'm sitting. Now what's going on?"

She hauled in a deep breath, searched his face, then blurted out, "I'm pregnant."

Fourteen years ago, those exact words had brought him to his knees and ripped his life apart. The effect was no different now.

Disbelief, rage, dread, and denial, mixed with a tiny drop of amazement, formed a tempest of uncertainty in his stomach. He closed his eyes and waited for his world to settle before he lashed out at Jade. Based on the fear in her eyes, she wasn't happy about the turn of events either. Or maybe she was afraid how he'd respond to the news.

"You said you were on the pill." The accusation hung heavy in the air. It took two to get pregnant, and he was the one who'd lost control and taken her without a condom.

"I was. But I got that stomach bug right after you left and couldn't keep anything down for forty-eight hours, including my contraceptive. Did you know that sperm can live up to five days in a woman's body? That was enough of a window... I googled it."

He digested that information. "How long have you known?"

"I did one of those home pregnancy tests on Monday. I've got a doctor's appointment tomorrow to confirm."

A baby. His baby. His worst nightmare. Another woman's future destroyed.

She reached over and grabbed his hand where it was fisted on the table next to his coffee cup. "I didn't do this deliberately, Harri. I know how hard this must be for you. I'm sorry."

She had no idea. She hadn't held her dead son in her arms. She hadn't watched the person she loved fade away, day by day, until there was nothing left to love. His guilt at not loving Emily in the end pricked at his heart every day, as if a vine full of thorns had grown in his chest, twisting and tearing at his organs with every movement.

"What are you going to do?" You, not we, as if it was only her problem. He pulled himself together. What the hell was wrong with him? "I'm sorry. I'm taking this badly. Can you give me a minute?"

He stood, battling the desire to run. He'd lived up to his responsibilities at eighteen. He'd just have to do it again at thirty-two.

"Eat your breakfast, have a shower, take all the time you want," Jade said. She'd also stood. In her bare feet, she barely reached his shoulder. So small, so delicate, so beautiful. She put a hand on his cheek, her gentle caress at odds with the emotion he was sure roared through her. Any normal man, upon hearing she carried his child, would have fallen at her feet and worshipped her. Was he too broken to fix?

She grabbed her handbag from where it had landed on the sofa last night and slipped on her heels from the wedding. "Just so you know, I don't expect or need anything from you. If you want nothing to do with me or the child, then that's okay. I can do this on my own."

"Jade…" He held his hand out but dropped it at his side when she moved away from him.

"If you want to see me again, I'll be at my flat."

The hotel room door *clicked* shut behind her, echoing the crack in his soul.

Chapter Sixteen

Jade closed her eyes in the backseat of the Uber but opened them again quickly when a vision of Harrison's stricken face filled her mind. He held the ball now, to either run with or pass. The decision was his. There was nothing she could do but wait.

If only it had just stayed a holiday affair. Even an unexpected pregnancy would be easier to deal with if all they had between them was lust. But no, she had to be a stupid fool and fall in love with the man.

The seedlings that had sprouted when he'd been so outraged at the comments made by the Indonesian businessmen had become full-fledged trees by the time she'd taken him to her house in Bali. The intervening weeks had proved it was more than an infatuation. She longed to hear his voice, feel the warmth of his hand in hers… Even a text message that made her laugh had been enough to keep her happy for a whole day. Jade Irvine was in love with Harrison Mackenzie.

And the best thing she could do at this point was walk out of his life for good.

The water in the kettle had just boiled when there was a commanding knock on her door. That he'd come didn't surprise her. That he'd come so quickly did. Was that a good sign? Or was he stopping by on his way to the airport?

"I was about to make a cup of tea. Would you like one?" she asked as she opened the door to him. *Let's pretend this is just a social call, and that my little announcement didn't destroy your life this morning.*

Harrison's hair was still damp and disheveled, but the rest of him looked all right. Gorgeous. The color was back in his face, and he even managed a small smile at her offer.

"I prefer coffee."

"Will instant do?"

He nodded, and she puttered around the kitchen making their drinks, avoiding the moment when she'd have to look in his eyes. Harrison would never walk away from what he considered his responsibility. Only she didn't want to be his responsibility. She wanted to be his love, the woman he cherished and cared for because he wanted to, not because he felt he had to.

"Um, I know this is a stupid question given all we have to talk about… It's just that my dad is expecting us for lunch, and if you're leaving, then … should I tell him we're not coming?" Nothing like destroying a man first thing on a Sunday morning then expecting him to come to lunch with her family.

"No, I should meet him properly. Will he expect a formal request for your hand in marriage?"

The words thrilled her, but she ruthlessly shut down her hope. The offer was prompted by his sense of responsibility, not love.

She crossed her arms over her chest to hold in her pounding heart. "First, I haven't told him about the baby. So he's not going to expect you to do the"—she put air quotes around the next two words—"honorable thing. Second, you can ask any way you want, but I'm not marrying you." If he'd said he loved her, she might consider it. But that didn't seem to be on the table right now. "I meant what I said at the hotel. I have a career, family, and friends. I can do this on my own. Harrison…" She waited until he looked at her and she softened her tone. "It's not the same situation as before. I'm not Emily."

"Don't say her name." His anguished voice silenced her. He raked a hand through his hair again, and she longed to settle the strands with her fingers.

Jade grabbed her cup and plopped herself on the sofa, hoping he'd join her. Instead, he paced across the room, six steps from door to window. It wasn't much of a stress reliever.

She sipped her tea to quell the rising nausea, wishing she'd grabbed a biscuit as well. As if reading her thoughts, Harrison grabbed the packet off the kitchen counter and passed it to her.

Finally, he said, "Let's start with the basics. Are you going through with the pregnancy?"

"Termination is not an option I will consider."

He sat then. "I'm glad." He took her hand in his. "I have to be a part of my child's life, Jade."

That stupid thing called hope grew a little stronger. If they stayed together, maybe love could grow in his heart. But until she knew he wanted her for her and not because she was the mother of his child, a formal commitment was not happening.

"There is a chance I may not be able to carry this baby to term. My mother had five miscarriages, two before me and three after. If I take after her…" Her voice broke on a sob. She'd only known she was pregnant for six days, but already she felt protective and loving toward her baby. This pregnancy may have been unplanned, but now that it was a reality, it wasn't unwanted.

He wrapped his arms around her and kissed the top of her head. "We'll deal with that if it happens. Together. But I need to plan for all possibilities."

She relaxed against him. His arms did make her feel safe and able to conquer mountains, even if he didn't love her enough to move them. "I bet your contingencies have contingencies," she said.

The first laugh of the day shook his chest. "There's nothing wrong with being prepared."

"You'd better be prepared enough for the two of us—make that the three of us—because I like to wing it most of the time."

He shifted her so her back was against his chest, his arms around her, one hand resting on her belly. She closed her eyes, committing the sensations coursing through her to memory. Peace. Joy. Love.

"We have to marry, Jade. It's the only logical solution." His words may have been spoken softly against her hair, but they still held a hint of command.

"It's the twenty-first century, Harri. Unmarried people have babies all the time. I'm not getting hitched to you just because you knocked me up. What happens if you fall in love in a year's time and find yourself stuck with me? I know you well enough that you'd let yourself be miserable, married to a woman you don't love, rather than end things to be with someone you do."

"I'm not going to fall in love."

Yeah, I already worked that one out for myself.

"You might. If you met a woman who helped you forget about your past…"

"How can I forget my past when it's repeating itself?"

Jesus, that hurt. She stood and faced him, her hands on her hips. "I. Am. Not. Emily."

He closed his eyes briefly and when he reopened them, the walls had returned. Harrison—lawyer, venture capitalist, stuck-up arse—was back in the room.

"All right. Even if we don't marry, I want to be a part of my child's everyday life. That means we need to live in the same country, preferably in the same house. My businesses are all based in Vancouver. I can't move to Australia, so you'll have to come to Canada. I'll check to see if it's possible for me to sponsor you, even if you're not my fiancée or my wife."

God, sometimes the man was insufferable. "Before you get on the Immigration Canada website, you might want to ask me if I'm willing to uproot my entire life and move to a different country. I don't need you, Harrison. My father is semi-retired and his new wife is fully retired. I'm sure if I ask, they'll be more than happy to look after the baby while I work. I have my career here, plus all my friends. Karly is pregnant as well. Our babies can grow up together and be best friends like their mothers. Why should I give all that up to move to a foreign country to live with a man who will never love me?"

He stood as well, towering over her. "And what am I supposed to do? Fly over to Australia every weekend to spend time with *my* child? I'm rich, remember. You won't need to work, or if you want to, we can hire nannies if my mother doesn't want to help out. And knowing her, when the baby arrives, you'll be lucky to get a cuddle in."

She took a deep, calming breath. She didn't want to argue with him. This should be a time of joy, a time of love. "There's no point fighting about this now. Let's have lunch and enjoy our weekend together. Next week, we can Skype each other and work out an interim plan then."

"You want to have this discussion from opposite sides of the earth?"

"Yes. I can't think straight when you're near."

He stepped closer and put a hand on her cheek, "Oh, really? Then I should press my advantage while I have it." His thumb rubbed along her lower lip, and she resisted the urge to lick him.

"I thought you said you'd never take advantage of me?"

"That was if you were drunk or sick. Right now, you're fair game." He lowered his head and his lips touched hers with an urgency that shook her to the core. Damn, the man weakened her knees with one touch. "Come back to Canada with me. At least check it out and meet my family," he said, his lips against her ear. "I'm sure you and my sister will be great friends."

When he asked like that…

She stepped back before she agreed to something stupid. "Tell you what. In six weeks, I'll be over the first trimester and will have a better idea if I can carry this baby to term." A cloud of pain swept through his eyes. "I'll come *visit* you then. It will be winter here, and I can enjoy some Canadian summer. You do have summer in Canada, don't you?"

"We have summer. Maybe not as hot as here, but nice enough."

"As long as I can wiggle my toes in the sand once a week, I'll survive. Are we agreed?"

"For now. Can I come to the doctor with you tomorrow?"

Whether it was the gentleness of his question or the awe that now shone in his eyes, it touched her deeply. "I'd like that."

He kissed her again. "We'd better go before we end up back in bed."

"Or tied to it," she added with a wink.

His eyes lit with desire. At least they had that.

And look where it had gotten them.

***

Harrison held the beer bottle by the neck and leaned against the stone half wall surrounding the backyard barbecue. His relaxed stance belied the turmoil inside him. Now that he'd had a few hours to get used to the idea of being a father once more, it rested easier on his shoulders ... until the blue face of his son flashed through his brain. Then his heart froze all over again. But things would be different this time. He wasn't living in a damp, cramped, illegal basement suite, and he could afford to hire people to monitor the baby twenty-four-seven.

He shifted to watch Jade surreptitiously while still facing her father. They'd arrived half an hour ago to the neat brick bungalow in one Melbourne's suburbs. The house was big but not ostentatious. It was the kind of place all the extended family would flock to on a Sunday afternoon for barbecue and beers. With the expanse of lawn and a tree perfect for a tire swing, it would be a great place for a small child. The thought knocked him back. Was he doing the right thing, insisting that Jade give up her life and come to Canada? There was no doubt that she could do this on her own and be a fantastic mother. What kind of dad was he going to be? Overprotective to the point of stifling, probably, given his history.

"At least you seem a damn sight better than the last bugger who came sniffing around my girl," Gordon said, noting Harrison's preoccupation with Jade.

Harrison took another swig of beer to chase down the taste of bile that had risen in his throat at the thought of another man with Jade. "Who was that?"

"A Pom scumbag who sold her the moon and when she went to collect, she found he already had a wife and child back in jolly old England. She packed up her life and chased after him only to have her heart crushed." Gordon pressed his spatula against a steak, making it sizzle on the grill. "You got a wife and kid hidden somewhere?"

"No. I'm a widower. My wife and son died over a decade ago."

Gordon took a healthy drink of his own beer before wiping the back of his hand across his mouth. "Sorry to hear that. When Dewi, my first wife, passed, I wanted to follow her to the grave. She was my everything. If I hadn't had Jade…" Gordon's gaze followed Harrison's over to Jade, who was laughing about something with her stepmother.

"Your daughter is definitely worth living for."

Gordon flipped the steaks. Seeming intent on his culinary task, Harrison was surprised at his next question. "At what point today are you going to tell me you've got her pregnant?"

Harrison choked on the beer he'd just swigged. "Sorry, what?"

"Can't fool me, boy." No one had called him "boy" in fourteen years. Not since he'd married and had a child. That didn't seem to matter to Jade's father. "Dewi was pregnant six times. You think I don't know the symptoms? From the day she turned eighteen, my daughter has rarely refused a drink if she's not driving. Now she's asking for soda water and sits at that table and nibbles on all the saltines but hasn't touched the goat cheese, which is her favorite? That girl is up the duff, and I'd bet my pension you're the one who got her there. Am I right?"

No point denying it. "Yes, sir." The memory of another conversation, when he confessed to a father that he'd gotten his daughter pregnant, how he'd do everything in his power to set it right, was eerily similar. Then, eighteen months later, he'd stared at the same man across the open grave of his daughter and acknowledged that he'd failed utterly. "I offered to marry her, but she refused."

"She did, huh?"

"Yes. She's worried that she'll miscarry and then be stuck in a marriage she doesn't want. But I can assure you, marriage or not, I'll look after her and the baby. Neither of them will ever want for anything."

"Except maybe a man around."

Harrison's chest felt like it could be on the grill next to the steaks. "That would be Jade's choice, not mine. I want to be as involved in my child's life as she'll let me."

Gordon's eyes snapped to his daughter again. "I'll tell you a secret. Jade's mother was pregnant when we married. Although that baby didn't survive, I never regretted the decision to marry her."

One confession deserved another. "My wife was also pregnant when we married. It didn't end so happily for us."

"Guess there's no guarantee. I never thought I'd love again after Dewi. But then Sandra walked into my life three years ago, and it was like the sun finally rose again. And I'll tell you, as an Aussie bloke, just saying things like that out loud to another man makes my kahunas shrivel, but it's the truth."

Harrison nodded and took another drag on his beer. He wasn't sure about testicle shrinkage, but something certainly happened whenever he looked at Jade.

"Jade tells me you used to play rugby." And with that, the conversation shifted to less personal topics and Harrison could relax. By the time they departed at seven thirty, his stomach was full, and a general buzz of contentment filled him.

"I'm … um … not sure where I'm going to sleep tonight," Jade said as they sat in the back of the Uber.

"You're sleeping with me. I didn't fly halfway around the world to sleep alone." They may be at odds about the future, but the present was cut and dried. He wanted her near him, any way he could get her.

"Shall we go back to my place, then? I believe it's your turn to do the walk of shame. Unless your sister sent another outfit for me to wear?"

"Men don't have a walk of shame. We strut with our head high and a goofy grin on our face so everyone knows we got lucky. And Sonia only sent the one dress. She must have figured that after one night, you'd be able to supply your own clothes. I'd prefer to go back to the hotel, though. It's a bit bigger."

"All right. But I still need to stop at my flat to grab a few things."

Jade gave the driver her address. While the car waited, Harrison accompanied her up the three flights of stairs to her apartment. There was no elevator. He'd be using that piece of knowledge to get her to move soon. Imagine doing that while heavily pregnant, or with a baby in her arms.

While Jade grabbed a few essentials, he examined the accommodations. He'd been too focused on her and the news of her pregnancy earlier to notice much. The apartment had one bedroom, and from a quick look, the double bed occupied ninety percent of the real estate, not leaving a lot of room for anything else. A sofa and coffee table took up most of the sitting room, and the small galley kitchen barely had enough space for a toaster and kettle. The place was tiny, slightly messy, but cheery. The walls and furniture were white, but splashes of color had been added with pillows and pictures. On the wall behind the sofa were a selection of framed photos of Jade and her friends in various locations doing silly things. It was the living space of a carefree single woman. But it wasn't big enough for a mother and child to live comfortably. Although at least it had running water and electricity.

They were back in the car within fifteen minutes, returning to the downtown core. Jade had snuggled against him, and he could tell from the weight of her body that she was exhausted.

He dropped a kiss on the top of her head. "I like your apartment, but it's going to be a pain dragging a baby stroller up three flights of stairs."

"Harrison." Her tone held a warning that she was not going to discuss this now.

"Just saying. By the way, your father knows our secret."

She sat up then. "No! How could he? Did you tell

him? Try and get him on your side?"

"Jade, your father is always going to be on your side. As he should be. But pregnancy symptoms are not a mystery to him."

"Shit. I should have known he'd twig, with the number of times my mum was pregnant. Why didn't he say anything to me?"

"He was probably waiting for you to tell him."

She sighed. "I'll call him tomorrow after the doctor's appointment. Do you still want to come with me?"

"More than anything." At the very least, he needed to know that Jade and the baby were well.

She leaned back against him. "My dad likes you."

"I like him, too."

Before he could say more, she was fast asleep. The mother of his child.

He ignored the alarm bells clamoring in his soul.

Chapter Seventeen

Harrison stood behind the railing at the Vancouver airport's international arrivals hall. His eyes were trained on the TV screens, waiting for his first glimpse of Jade. Although he'd seen her almost daily via Skype for the past six weeks, he couldn't wait to hold her in his arms again.

He still wasn't quite sure what to make of his obsession with her. It was different from what he'd felt for Emily. That had been a gentle, peaceful feeling—at least until her addiction had spiraled out of control. With Jade, it was all-consuming, passionate, unsettling. Every morning he woke with a knot in his stomach, wondering if this would be the day she said she wanted nothing more to do with him.

Until then, he prepared for their life together. He hoped she liked his surprise.

A woman with a long black braid, a floaty flower-print top, and white jeans appeared on the screen, and his heart rate sped up.

"Fancy meeting you here."

His gaze shot from the screen to his sister standing next to him. "What the hell, Sonia?"

"I figured you were going to keep her in your bed for the next week, and I'd never get a chance to meet the mystery woman who has you giggling in the middle of meetings. This may be my only chance."

"I will pay you two million dollars to go away right now." He hadn't told anyone about the baby, and although he doubted Jade was showing yet, at only three months, he wasn't going to risk her saying something that would alert his sister to the situation.

"Two million? That's chump change for you."

"I'll accidentally email photos of you and that guy you picked up in the nightclub last week to Mom." Blackmail worked both ways.

Sonia shrugged, but he noticed the tension in her shoulders. "I picked him up for Mandy."

He dared a glance down the hallway. Jade would walk through the doors any second, and he wanted Sonia gone. "Mandy is pretty enough to get her own men."

"Yeah, but she's shy. And what were you doing there, spying on me?"

"Two of my clients were there and recognized you. They snapped the photo, since the guy you snagged was wearing one of their shirts."

"Likely story."

He did not have time for this. "Go, Sonia. I promise you can have lunch with Jade tomorrow."

"All right, then." With a quick kiss on his cheek, she turned and strode away.

He turned back to the walkway to find Jade standing directly in front of him. Her face was a bit pale. "Who was that?"

"My sister. To make her go away, I promised she could meet you at lunch tomorrow."

She smiled, and his chest suddenly felt lighter. "Good to know I'll be allowed out of your bed by noon." She reached up and pulled his head down for a kiss. But with the barrier between them, it left a lot to be desired.

"Or maybe Sonia can talk to you through the closed door while I trail chocolate covered strawberries down your naked body."

Her voice was breathless when she replied, "That works for me too."

He leapt over the barrier, ignoring the stern look from the security guard, and pulled her properly into his arms. "God, I missed you."

"How far away is your flat?"

Laughter burst from his chest. This woman made him feel things he'd never experienced before. He had to make her stay. "Not far. You must be tired after your flight." He put one arm around her waist, which was still as small as it had been before, grabbed her bag, and headed toward the door.

She smiled up at him, and his chest tingled. "Yeah, tired. Let's go with that excuse for ending up in bed. You've spoiled me, you know, sending me first class. Economy will never be the same again. I slept most of the way. Which means I've got lots of energy now."

He opened his mouth to say she need never fly economy class again, but closed it. There were better ways to persuade her to marry him than luxury travel. "Good, because I've got plans for you."

Wishing now that he'd hired a limo to take them

home, he led her to his car. If he hadn't had to drive, he could have held her in the back, maybe caress a bit of skin revealed by her loose top, steal a kiss or two… Driving a stick shift with a boner was no fun.

"Nice ride," Jade said.

He opened the passenger door of his Aston Martin Vanquish and waited for Jade to get comfortable. She shimmied in the seat, sending heat straight to his groin. Definitely a limo next time. "If you like, I'll take you up to Whistler. This car was made for a road like the Sea to Sky Highway."

As they drove to his condo in the city, Jade kept him amused with stories about her friends and their reaction to her pregnancy. "Lauren swears she knew at the wedding that something was up, but she was too distracted by your kilt to say anything."

"Ah yes, the old kilt distraction technique. Unfortunately, I don't think it will work on my sister at lunch tomorrow."

"You haven't told your family?"

"No. I…"

"Don't worry, I understand. The only reason I've told people is because my not drinking alcohol was a dead giveaway. Besides, we wanted to be sure…"

She didn't mention the possibility of miscarriage, and he was grateful. Every day, he'd feared she'd phone to tell him the worst had happened. But all had been well at her twelve-week check-up, so he'd finally relaxed. A little.

He reached over and took her hand in his. "I've booked an ultrasound at a private clinic. I'd like to see our baby."

"Sounds perfect. What else do you have planned?"

"Outside the bedroom?"

Her sexy laughed filled the car, and he pressed the accelerator a little too hard, almost launching them into the back of a bus. He needed to concentrate more on driving and less on the idea of Jade naked.

"I have a special dinner arranged for us tonight. Then lunch tomorrow with my sister. Once that happens, dinner with my parents will inevitably follow. We could take a trip to Whistler on Sunday, if you're up for it. Then next week is open except for the ultrasound on Monday morning."

He pulled into the underground parking at his condo building. As he maneuvered into his double-wide spot—a perk of owning a penthouse suite—he glanced over at his business partner and neighbor's spot. Caleb's SUV was gone. They had probably headed out for the weekend. Malee, Caleb's wife, wasn't fond of the city, so they spent as much time as possible out of it. At least that would give Jade some time to settle in before he introduced them. Malee was in her last month of pregnancy, so the two women would probably want to compare notes. Harrison wasn't looking forward to Caleb's teasing about getting things ass-backward again. But considering the rock his friend had been during Harrison's disastrous marriage, he'd put up with it and smile.

The ride in the elevator to his floor was conducted in silence. But he noticed that Jade's skin was flushed, and her breath came in uneven pants.

"Are you okay?" he asked as he opened the door to his place. He pulled her suitcase in behind him, and by the time he'd shut the door and turned, she'd already discarded her shirt and was tugging off her jeans.

"The one thing they neglect to tell you about pregnancy is how incredibly horny it makes you. At least Karly has Hugh on tap. I had to fly seventeen hours to get my fix." Her underpants followed her jeans, and then her bra joined the rest of her clothes in his foyer. Her dark nipples were already peaked, jutting toward him, calling him…

"Harrison, is that you?" his mother's voice iced over the lust flowing through his veins at Jade's disrobing. "Your father had an appointment at St. Paul's this morning, so we stopped in here for a coffee before we headed back home. What are you doing off work so early?"

His mother emerged from the kitchen at the same time as Jade jumped behind his back with a squeal.

"Oh, sorry, I didn't know you had…" His mother looked at the trail of clothes on the floor and then at him. "Um … company." He was a big man, but it was impossible to hide a naked woman entirely.

His father appeared a second later, his cane nowhere in sight. He took in the scene, and when his gaze met Harrison's, it was full of unholy mirth. "You were right, Sue," his dad said. "This is so much better than getting coffee at Starbucks."

"Mom, Dad, this is Jade Irvine. Jade, please meet

Hamish and Seung Mackenzie, my parents."

Jade's head appeared around his right side. "Pleased to meet you. Excuse me if I don't shake hands."

His father burst into laughter, while his mother scurried from the room to return a moment later with his bathrobe in hand, which she tossed to him from a distance. Unfortunately, his mother had the throwing skills of a one-eyed T-rex, and it landed about three feet away. He didn't dare move to retrieve it. "We'll wait for you on the balcony," his mother said, her voice unnaturally high. "It's such a beautiful day, shame to waste the sunshine. We don't see enough of it sometimes…" Her voice trailed off as she grabbed his father's arm and dragged him out onto the terrace.

When he was sure his parents were gone, he snagged the robe and handed it to Jade. She tugged it on with jerky movements. "Oh God, what must your parents think of me?"

He took her face between both his hands and kissed her lips, lingering in the embrace. "My father is thinking his son is the luckiest man in Vancouver, possibly Canada. And my mother is wondering if it's too early to start looking at wedding venues. They're cool people, Jade. Now hold your head high and come meet them properly."

With her hand in his, he led her toward the balcony off the kitchen, from where he could hear his mother's voice. How fast could he get rid of his parents and reclaim his bathrobe?

***

She was going to title this episode "How *Not* to Meet the Boyfriend's Parents" and pretend it had happened in a sitcom and not to her personally. At least, as Harrison had said, his parents seemed pretty cool about it. As she stepped onto the large balcony, his mother's gaze never drifted below her chin, and his father's blue eyes were so full of laughter, it made her want to smile too.

With a deep breath, she squared her shoulders and held out her hand to Hamish. "Right. Introductions, take two. I'm Jade Irvine. Pleased to meet you."

She shook Hamish's hand, so like his son's. In fact, aside from their coloring, the two men were almost identical. They were the same height and build, but Hamish had reddish-blond hair, and there was no mistaking the source of Harrison's incredible blue eyes. The only sign that he'd had health issues recently was an abandoned cane leaning against the sun lounger, and the left side of his mouth didn't go quite as high when he smiled. "You're a bonny lass, and I'm happy to meet you." His Scottish burr was charming, but it didn't have the same effect on her as when his son used it.

"Please call me Sue," Harrison's mother said as she approached with her hand outstretched. The woman was tiny, five feet if anything. Her slender frame was the opposite of her husband and son. Harrison had inherited his black hair from her, and the Korean heritage that was hinted at in the son was in full force in the mother. Unmissable, however, was the obvious love she had for Harrison. Jade felt a twinge, wishing her own mother were still around. Especially now that she was going to become a parent herself.

"Sorry about that." Jade waved a hand back toward the foyer.

"Not at all. We're the ones who are here uninvited," Hamish said. "Speaking of which, we should get going, Sue, before the traffic gets bad." He put his half-full coffee cup on the table and stood. There was a hint of fatigue in his eyes, and he leaned heavily on the table when getting to his feet.

"Yes, yes, of course." Sue put her cup down as well, even though it looked like she hadn't touched it yet. "It was nice to meet you, Jade."

Jade didn't want them leaving on her account. "There's no need—"

"Mom, how about we come for dinner tomorrow night?" Harrison wrapped both arms around Jade from behind, trapping her against his hard body.

A bright smile lit his mother's face. "Yes, that would be lovely. See you tomorrow, Jade."

Hamish clapped his son on the back as he stepped past him. "Carry on, son," he said. "Nice to meet you, Jade."

She waited until she heard the front door close behind his parents before she turned in Harrison's arms and buried her face against his chest. "That was … epic."

Harrison chuckled and lifted her face with a thumb under her chin. "It will certainly give them something to talk about on the drive home. But don't worry about them. Finally, I can greet you properly."

He lowered his head for a kiss, but she pulled out of his arms and walked back into the flat. It was an amazing space. One complete wall was windows overlooking an inlet and the mountains across the shore. And she knew just the way she wanted to admire the view.

"Here should do." She dropped the robe and put her hands on the back of the sofa, in a perfect position to admire the scenery while Harrison rogered her from behind.

"Jade?"

She looked over her shoulder. "Why do you still have your clothes on?"

He picked up the robe and placed it over her. "This is not what we are, Jade."

Her heart shrank in her chest. If they didn't have sex, what did they have? Her body hadn't changed that much with pregnancy yet. If anything, her boobs were bigger. Why did he no longer want her? She put her arms in the sleeves and refastened the robe with jerky movements.

"What are we, then?"

He ran a hand through his hair. "We're not just casual sex. For God's sake, Jade, six months from now we're going to be parents."

"And would-be parents don't have sex?"

"Not like this."

"How do they do it, then?"

He caressed her cheek with one hand and pulled

her closer with the other. "Gentle kisses easing into passion. Soft caresses leading to a reverential exploration of the body. I want to make love to you, Jade—worship your changing body. Not take you over the back of the sofa like a barbarian."

His lips too briefly flitted across hers before trailing kisses along her jaw and then down her throat. His words had touched a place inside her she hadn't known existed. Hope raised its naïve head within her before she forcefully stomped it down. Just because he was a fabulous lover didn't mean he *loved* her. He slipped an arm behind her knees and next thing she knew, she was being carried toward what she hoped was his bedroom.

She wasn't going to ruin their reunion wishing for something he wouldn't give her. "So over the sofa is off the agenda?"

His deep chuckle echoed into her heart. "No, just further down the order of business. I've wanted you in my bed for months now, and that's where we're heading."

He kicked open a wood-paneled door and she had a brief glimpse at a navy-blue-and-burgundy-styled room before it all spun out of control. As promised, Harrison worshipped her body, bringing her to the edge of climax twice before he entered her. When he finally shifted to lay beside her, both were covered in perspiration, and she doubted her legs would ever work again.

She wasn't sure how long she dozed, but she woke to Harrison drawing lazy circles around her enlarged nipples. "We'd better shower and dress for dinner."

"Can't we stay here?" She stretched, rubbing her body against his deliberately.

"No. I have a surprise for you, and I can't wait any longer."

After an all-too-brief shower, they drove through the streets of Vancouver, then along the waterfront past some cute little shops and restaurants. It was just the kind of place Jade would love to explore on foot at her leisure. "What's this area?"

"Point Grey. It's also home to Jericho Beach, which I'm sure you'll enjoy." The road split in two and Harrison veered to the right. Within minutes, they were driving along a wide expanse of beach, with huge houses nestled against the face of the cliff on the other side of the road. Harrison parked his beautiful car and turned to her. "Walk on the beach or surprise first?"

"Surprise."

He leaned over and kissed her lightly. "I'm glad you said that. I wasn't sure how much longer I could wait."

They got out of the car, and he took her hand and led her across the street and up the steps to a white stone house, the front of which was almost all glass. Harrison pulled a key from his pocket and opened the door, ushering her inside.

"Whose place is this?" She glanced around. Although decorated mostly in white, there were splashes of reds and oranges that gave it a warm, homey feel. The open-plan concept made it feel airy and bright. It was a beautiful home, but she wasn't sure why he'd brought her here … unless it was to have dinner with his friends. In which case, she was definitely going to keep her clothes on.

"Let's have a look around first." They wandered through the various spaces. The kitchen was particularly beautiful, with folding glass doors that opened out onto a walled garden. There was a laundry room and an elevator that Harrison said ran from the downstairs garage. The second floor held two large bedrooms, both with ensuite bathrooms, and a large, spacious office.

Harrison took her hand and led her up to the third floor. They looked first into a cheery room set up as a nursery. A tingle went up Jade's spine, but she wouldn't let herself run her finger over the mahogany crib. Next door, through a connecting bathroom, was a cute child's bedroom.

The master suite took up almost the whole front of the house and, if possible, the view from there was even better than it was at his flat. From the balcony, she could see the beach and ocean, Vancouver's downtown core, and the mountains beyond. She sucked in a deep breath and enjoyed the fresh air.

"It's beautiful. Is it your friend Caleb's place?" Harrison had often talked about Caleb and his Thai wife, Malee, during their nightly conversations. She was looking forward to meeting them. But they mustn't have moved in yet, because the house lacked any personal touches.

"No, it's ours. I knew you'd like it."

A chill swept through her. He was taking over, not giving her a choice. "Our place? How do *we* have a place? You have a place, and I have a place, but so far, there's no *we* to have a place."

"Then it's your place. You and the baby can live here, and I'll stay in my condo in Coal Harbour."

Her stomach fell to her knees. It hadn't even been six hours, and he was pressuring her already. "I'm not moving to Canada."

He scrubbed both hands over his face, and she could hear his frustration in the tone of his voice. "Jade, I can't move to Australia. If I have to, I will fight you for custody of our child. But I'd rather work with you and come to a mutually agreeable solution. I've asked you to marry me, and you said no. If you don't want to cohabit, then we can at least live in the same city."

"Harri—" A stabbing pain sliced through her lower abdomen, doubling her over, forcing all the breath from her body. Attempting to pull in more air only increased the agony. When she said his name a second time, it was full of panic. "Harrison! The baby!"

Chapter Eighteen

Please, God. Not again. Harrison held Jade's hand tightly, and by sheer willpower, forced back the dark memories threatening to consume him. Her face was ghostly white, her emerald eyes huge. "Are you still in pain?" He couldn't fail this baby as he had Bryce. He couldn't fail Jade.

"No. It's eased now. But my heart is running a mile a minute."

"Probably just the stress. It'll be okay, babe. The nurse said it was most likely ligament pain from your expanding uterus."

"Then why am I still in the hospital?"

He'd carried Jade into Women's and Children's Hospital and basically promised them an entire new wing if they would see her immediately.

"They want to run some tests to make sure everything's normal." He'd insisted. While the ER doctor had done a cursory examination, Harrison wanted everything checked.

He'd also called Caleb and asked for the name of Malee's obstetrician. Caleb had called the doctor himself and within twenty minutes, the physician had arrived. And for the first time since Jade had screamed in pain, Harrison had been able to draw a deep breath. The man exuded calm and competence. After a brief examination, he'd gone off to find the test results. But before departing, he'd said that since there was no bleeding, which usually accompanied a miscarriage, it was likely that all was well. Harrison held onto that glimmer of hope.

"If I lose the baby, there'll be no need for that beautiful house." A tear slid down Jade's face, and he wiped it away with his thumb.

He smiled to reassure her. "I knew you liked the house."

"It's beautiful. And right by the beach."

"You told me you could never live far from the sand."

"And you the mountains."

"That's why Vancouver is perfect for both of us."

"Harri…" Exhaustion obscured the warning in her voice that she did not want to get into this now.

"I know, bad timing. Can't help it. I'm a lawyer at heart, and I always press my advantage when I see an opening."

The doctor pushed open the curtain and entered the cubicle. Harrison tried to read his expression, but the man's face was a blank mask.

"How are you feeling now, Ms. Irvine?" the doctor asked.

"Better. Is the baby okay?"

"Your baby is fine. You're not having a miscarriage."

Jade squeezed Harrison's hand and a couple more tears escaped. Her obvious love for their unborn child made his chest tighten.

"Then what was the pain?" she asked.

"As your baby grows, your body might protest the changes. Some pain is natural as things stretch and move within you. However, your situation seems to have been exacerbated by dehydration, elevated blood pressure, and low blood sugar. I will discharge you if you promise to go home, have something to eat, drink plenty of water, and stay in bed for the next twenty-four hours."

The doctor looked at him, and Harrison nodded. God, he was such an idiot. Jade had come off a very long flight and rather than care for her, he'd had sex with her then dragged her around town. Some responsible adult he was.

"But we're supposed to go to your parents for dinner tomorrow night," Jade said as the doctor wrote some notes on her chart.

He looked up from what he was writing. "If you feel absolutely one hundred percent and don't do anything too strenuous, then I don't see that dinner will be a problem. Who is your regular obstetrician?"

"She's in Australia. I just arrived in Vancouver this afternoon."

"Then I would like to follow up with you on Monday to make sure your blood pressure and other vitals have returned to normal." The doctor turned to Harrison. "Caleb Doyle said you would make a very generous contribution to the hospital if I saw Ms. Irvine immediately. I assume you will also cover her medical expenses while she's in Canada, if she's not insured?"

"I will."

"Very good. Call my office first thing Monday and tell them I said to squeeze you in late afternoon." He handed Harrison a card then turned back to Jade. "Welcome to Canada. Don't worry, we're going to take very good care of you and your baby."

"Thank you, doctor," both he and Jade said at once.

The doctor left, and the nurse bustled in and unhooked Jade from the IV drip. When she was dressed, he insisted on carrying her out to the car then up to his condo.

"What would you like to eat?" he asked after settling her in bed. All the energy had been drained from him, and he wanted nothing more than to lie down and pretend the nightmare of the past four hours hadn't happened. The reminder about how quick life could change had hit him like a sledgehammer.

"Some scrambled eggs and a bit of toast. And a cup of tea, if you have any."

He hurried out to get her dinner, bringing her a glass of water first to help her rehydrate. When he returned, she was dozing, and he took a second to absorb her beauty. A small smile curved her lips upward, as though she dreamed of something pleasant.

Setting the tray down on the bedside table, he sat on the bed and brushed his knuckles over her cheek. Her eyelids fluttered open, and the air in his lungs whooshed out.

"You need to eat before you sleep, babe. Shall I feed you?"

"I can feed myself. But I'd like you to sit with me and tell me what I can see out the window."

Dusk was settling in, and the lights from the suburbs across the inlet sparkled in the early summer evening. He pointed out some of the sights and talked about places he'd like to take her. When she finished eating, he piled the dishes up on the tray and went to take them into the kitchen.

"You are coming back, aren't you?" She wiggled against the pillow, and heat flooded his groin. For God's sakes, the woman had just come out of the hospital and he was hot for her again?

"I'll sleep in the guest bedroom tonight. I don't want to disturb you."

"It will disturb me more to know we're under the same roof and you're not next to me. I'm not going to break because you sleep in the same bed."

"You're under doctor's orders to rest, Jade."

"I promise to keep my hands to myself. You blame yourself for this afternoon, don't you?"

"Of course I do. It was my fault. You spent seventeen hours traveling here, and I didn't even offer you a glass of water."

She was shaking her head before he'd even finished. "I'm a grown woman, Harri. I was the one who forgot to eat and drink. It's not up to you to look after me."

"Yes, it is."

She sat up and crossed her arms over her chest. "It's a good thing for you that I'm under doctor's orders to stay in bed. Otherwise I'd get up and whoop your arse for such stupidity. I can take care of myself. Now, if you're not in this bed when I wake up, I'll go and find you. Then it *will* be on your head that I'm out of bed."

"All right. I just have a couple of calls to make, then I'll be in."

He called Sonia and put off lunch the next day instead inviting her to dinner at their parents. Then he phoned Caleb and brought him up to speed on what had happened. Seeing as he hadn't even told his best friend and partner about the baby, the request for an obstetrician had been a bit of a shock. But if anyone knew how to go with the flow, it was Caleb.

When he returned to the bedroom a couple of hours later, Jade was fast asleep. Something was so right about climbing into bed next to her. But this afternoon had shown him how quickly it could all be taken away.

Could he put himself through that again? Would he go insane, worried every second that something would happen to one or both of them? What choice did he have?

The only way he was going to get through this was if he controlled every variable possible. Jade was about to find out just how pole-up-the-ass he could be.

***

Jade woke to a pale pink light slipping through the half-closed blinds. A large hand rested on her hip, and the heat of another body warmed her back. Even better, the nausea that usually greeted her every day was absent. She shifted toward the edge of the bed, and Harrison came instantly awake.

"Where are you going?" His sleep-filled voice was so sexy.

"To the loo. Go back to sleep."

He threw back the blankets. "I'll carry you."

"Harri, I can make it to the bathroom and back on my own."

"But the baby—"

"Is just fine. Remember? If you want to be useful, you can make me a cup of tea."

He looked undecided for a moment, then went off to the kitchen while she escaped to the loo. One look in the mirror showed her why Harrison was so concerned. She looked like she'd been dragged backward through a bush, twice.

When she emerged from the bathroom fifteen minutes later, she felt like a new woman. But from the scowl on Harrison's face, it hadn't helped.

"You locked the door," he said.

"Uh, yeah, I was doing stuff I didn't want to be disturbed doing."

"What if you'd passed out? Don't lock the door again."

Only the haggard expression on his face stopped her from telling him where he could stick his lock. He probably hadn't slept all night, worried about her and the baby.

"While I appreciate your concern, this overprotectiveness is going to get old fast." She walked toward the bedroom door, but he moved to block her way.

"Bed rest for twenty-four hours. Doctor's orders."

"But I feel great."

"Jade."

"Oh, all right. But if I have to stay here, so do you."

A relieved smile curved his lips. "Agreed. Your tea is on the bedside table. I'll be back in a minute with breakfast."

She crawled back in bed, discovered the remote to open the blinds, and then sipped her tea as she admired the day dawning over Vancouver. It was her first trip to Canada, and she itched to explore.

Harrison returned with a massive tray holding six different breakfast items.

"You don't expect me to eat all that, do you?"

"As much as you can. I researched pregnancy diets last night while you slept."

She munched on a slice of whole wheat toast. "What else did you do?"

"Aside from watch you? I looked up the risks of high blood pressure and the other things the doctor mentioned. This is serious, Jade." He looked away briefly, and when his gaze met hers again, she sucked in a breath. Sheer torment clouded his gorgeous blue eyes. "If you develop preeclampsia, you and the baby could die."

The anguish in his voice tugged at her heart. She patted the bed beside her. "I'm sure yesterday was just an anomaly brought on by the flight and me being overexcited. But I promise you that I will follow all the doctor's orders to the letter. I want this baby, Harri, very much." She rubbed her lower belly then reached over and squeezed his hand.

"Jade, will you marry me?"

Her heart thrilled to hear his words. "Why?"

"Why? Because you're carrying my child and I want to look after you both, share my life and my wealth, be a family."

"What about love?"

He ran a hand through his hair. "I care for you deeply. And I will love our child, I promise. But I'm not sure I have it in me to love a woman."

"Your heart still belongs to Emily." He would never know what it cost her to say those words.

He got up from the bed and moved over to the window. He stared out for several long minutes and Jade didn't think he would refute her comment. She'd lost her appetite but forced down some yogurt and fruit for the baby's sake.

"I didn't love Emily at the end. I hated that she'd chosen drugs over me, that the beautiful, sweet girl I married had become an addict." He turned, and she could see the pain in his eyes. "When I found her on the kitchen floor, do you know what my first thought was? It was, "Thank God it's over." What kind of monster sees his eighteen-year-old wife dead and feels relief? You don't want my love, Jade. It's toxic."

Without waiting for her response, he strode from the room.

The pain that seared through her this time had

nothing to do with her pregnancy. She could marry a man she loved but who didn't love her. Or she could go back to Australia, forget about Harrison—a near impossibility, since he insisted on being a part of his child's life—and eventually find a decent guy who would love her and her child. Her father had dared to love again. She would as well.

As soon as the doctor cleared her to leave, she was heading back to Australia.

***

"She's a lovely girl," his mother said as she stirred the gravy. "So bright and bubbly and yet mature too. I like her."

"Even though you found her without clothes yesterday?"

"Let's just say if your father didn't have health issues, I might have done the same when we came home."

"Eww, mom. I did not want to hear that."

His mother stuck her tongue out at him. "I didn't find you in a kimchi jar, you know. You were made the traditional way. I'm not judging a woman with strong passions."

He put down the knife that he'd been using to slice the chicken. In the other room, Jade and his father were yelling at the rugby game on TV. "She's pregnant." His mother turned to him then, the spoon frozen in her hand. "And yes, it's mine."

"Oh." She resumed stirring, but there was a

jerkiness to her movements that indicated her anxiety. "I'm not going to lecture you. I'm sure you've already done that yourself."

He nodded. "I've asked her to marry me, but she's refused."

"Smart woman."

"Mom?"

"Harrison, don't do this again. Don't marry a woman just because she's having your baby." The anguish in his mother's voice ripped a hole in his heart.

"Two seconds ago, you said you liked her."

"I do. But I love you. Your marriage to Emily was a disaster, and it almost took you away from us. Every day, I worried she'd lure you into drugs."

"Jade is not going to lure me into drugs."

"Whatever. I don't want you marrying her."

His mother's attitude surprised him. He thought she'd be ecstatic to discover she was about to become a grandmother again.

"Don't say anything to Jade, please. She was in the hospital yesterday and she's supposed to be on bedrest. But she insisted on coming to dinner tonight."

His mother stopped stirring. "Is everything okay with the baby?"

"The baby's fine. It's Jade. Her blood pressure is high and her blood sugar is low. I need to make sure she eats regularly and stays calm."

"And proposing is your way of keeping her calm?"

God, what was it with women? Weren't they

usually clamoring for a marriage proposal? The way Jade and his mother responded, it was as if he was asking if they wanted to share his cold. "I want to get it settled. I've bought a house in Point Grey near the beach. The baby is my responsibility, and I'll live up to that."

"And I'm sure you mentioned that during your marriage proposal as well."

"Maybe. Why?"

"Because no woman wants to be considered a responsibility." She poured the gravy into a white ceramic dish and nodded at the chicken on her way to the dining room. "Bring that through when you're done carving."

Sonia burst through the door as his mother reentered the kitchen. "Sorry I'm late." Her eyes narrowed, seeing the expression on their mother's face. "What's happened? Is Dad okay?"

"Your brother has again gotten a girl pregnant, she's refused to marry him, and we're not to talk about it," his mother said. She pulled a platter out of the cupboard and started arranging the roasted vegetables. Nothing like a little passive-aggressive guilt trip to go with dinner.

"Really? Sounds like the most interesting dinner conversation we've had since the last time he got a girl preggers."

"Shut up, Sonia. I don't want Jade upset."

"Oh my God. I'm pregnant?" Jade leaned against the doorframe, a mischievous smile on her face. "How'd that happen?" She turned to his sister and held out her hand. "Happy to meet you, Sonia. I'm your brother's pregnant lover. But you can call me Jade."

The two women shook hands, smiles on both their faces. He knew they'd get along.

He wiped his hands on a towel and walked over to Jade. "You're supposed to bc resting."

"I'm fine. Australia beat Scotland, so I'm giving Hamish a chance to cry in private."

"I'm not crying," his father yelled from the other room.

"I'm pregnant," Jade called back.

His father appeared in the doorway and wrapped his arm around Jade's shoulders. "Congratulations, lassie," he said, although the look he sent Harrison was anything but congratulatory.

Jade put her arm around his dad's waist. "Finally, someone who's happy I'm having a baby."

"We're all happy, dear," his mother said, her voice brittle. "Just a bit concerned after last time."

Jade released his dad and crossed her arms. "It's not going to be like last time. I'm not a sixteen-year-old high school student with no decent family to support her. I'm not going to become a drug addict, and I sure as hell don't need looking after. I'm twenty-six, and I have a good job and a stable family. I want this baby and will love it with everything I've got."

"Two stable families now, love." His father dropped a kiss on her head. "We're here for you as well."

Sonia gave Jade a hug, pushing Harrison out of the way. "Do you know if it's a boy or girl yet?"

"Not yet. We're scheduled for a sonogram Monday morning, but it might be too early to tell. I've heard you have to be closer to twenty weeks. I'm only thirteen."

"Well, as soon as you know, tell me. I'm going to convince Mandy to design a range of baby outfits. My niece or nephew can be the first to model them."

Harrison moved his sister out of the way and wrapped his arms around Jade again. The need to hold her was becoming a problem. "My baby is not going to be an instrument for your friend to further her fashion career."

"*Our* career, you mean. I was going to announce this at dinner, but seeing as we've already got something to talk about… I don't want to go into property development. I'm opening a fashion house with Mandy. Dad's business is all yours, big brother."

The clock on the living room mantel was the only sound in the stunned silence.

He did not need full control of his father's business empire in addition to his own. Neither could he deny his sister her dream.

He was now well and truly tied to Canada. He had no choice but to convince Jade to stay.

Chapter Nineteen

"Can you tell the baby's gender?" Jade asked, as the ultrasound technician pressed the transducer into her lower abdomen.

"Not definitively, and I wouldn't want to say either way. Six more weeks and it should be clear. The baby looks healthy. All the measurements are where they should be for thirteen weeks, and the heart is strong. Would you like the photos?"

"Yes. Two sets, please," Harrison said. He hadn't taken his eyes off the screen once since the test had begun. But he'd squeezed Jade's hand tight when they saw the heart beating fast and regular. She'd glanced at his face, and it had been filled with awe.

The technician pressed a couple more buttons on her machine and then wiped the jelly off Jade's stomach.

Harrison finally released her hand and helped her sit up. If she changed position too quickly, she got dizzy. "The appointment with the doctor is at three thirty. Do you want to go back to the condo to rest or get some lunch?"

"Sonia is going to meet me at your flat, and then we're going to grab a bite. I assumed you'd have to get to work."

"I'd planned to work from home today between

appointments. I'm glad you and Sonia hit it off Saturday night."

Dinner had been awkward to say the least, but she hadn't been able to tell whether it was her announcement or Sonia's that had put the real damper on the evening. Hamish's gaze had darted between his children, and the sadness in his eyes had tugged at her heart. She hadn't meant to dismiss Harrison's family from her future child's life. She'd just wanted to reassure them that she wasn't going to bring Harri down with her. Sue had kept her eyes on her plate, rarely raising her head. When she did, her smile was fake. Thank God Harrison had claimed Jade was still jetlagged and they had to leave early. True enough, even though she'd spent the day in bed, she had been tired. Maybe there was something wrong with her. That was another reason she didn't want the Mackenzie family to get too attached to her—they'd had enough heartbreak already.

On Sunday, they'd had a lazy day, just her and Harrison, who had treated her like she was made of eggshells. After a leisurely breakfast, they'd taken a drive around Stanley Park and up Cypress Mountain to see the view of the city and beyond. They'd even walked on the beach at English Bay and had ice cream at a shop reputed to have five hundred flavors. She'd ordered coconut ginger, since her nausea had threatened to return at the idea of eating curry, asparagus, or wasabi-flavored ice cream. In the evening, they'd cooked a simple meal together and then sat on the terrace of his apartment and chatted until the sun went down. It had been a perfect day. If only he'd say he loved her, she'd stay.

But he hadn't, so she couldn't.

Harrison took the photos from the technician, thanked her, and held Jade's hand on the way out to the car. She could get used to this kind of service.

Talking about Sonia was easier than talking about their situation, so she said, "I like your sister. She's fun."

"Fun? Another word for Sonia is immature. Two years ago, she said she wanted to take over Dad's company. So I went into partnership with Caleb. Then, when Dad got sick, it accelerated the timeline and I agreed to help in the transition. Now she's throwing it all away for some half-assed idea of setting up a fashion house. Do you know what the competition is like in that industry? If she even manages to turn a profit in the next five years, she'll be swallowed alive by the big fish."

"Don't you think your sister deserves a shot at doing something she's passionate about?"

"At what cost? My mom is terrified that Dad will go back to work full time and have another stroke. Dad is worried that if he doesn't retake the helm, the company will fold and all his employees, some of whom have been with him since the start, will be out of work."

"And you?"

He drove out of the parking lot and merged into traffic. "Me?"

"What are you worried about?"

He pulled over to the curb and stopped the car. "I'm worried that Dad will go back to work and it will be too much for him. I'm worried that Mom will crack under the pressure. I'm worried that Sonia will put all her energy into this business and end up with nothing. I'm worried that this pregnancy will be too hard on your body and either you or the baby will die, maybe both of you. And it will all be my fault. Every last goddamned bit of it."

Her heart ached for the pressure he put himself under. She reached over and laced her fingers with his. "How is any of this your fault?"

"Dad just had a regular construction company until the thing with Emily. Then he figured he needed to step it up to leave a legacy for his grandson. He pushed himself hard and ruined his health. Mom was devastated when Bryce died, and after Emily … well, she had to quit work. Her nerves were never the same. Emily had been like a big sister to Sonia, so after her death, we all sheltered Sonia. She has no idea what the real world is like. And you … well, that's self-explanatory."

"I'm not going to comment on what happened before with your family, except to say that Sonia may yet surprise you. Her friend Mandy designed that dress you brought me in Australia, and it was a huge hit. At least twenty people asked me where I got it. My friend Lauren has a boutique and is always looking for original designs. I'm sure she'd love to carry Sonia and Mandy's pieces."

"One shop in Australia is not going to make their

company profitable."

"No, it won't. But Sonia has the passion to make it work." The bigger issue was him thinking he was solely responsible for her pregnancy. "I'll be damned, though, if I let you take the blame for my pregnancy. I was there, remember. At any point I could have told you to stop and get a condom. But I didn't, because I loved the feeling of having you inside me. Just you, no barriers, nothing between us but passion. And I don't regret it. You've given me the greatest gift a man can give a woman. And I don't care what it takes. If I have to spend the next six months flat on my back, I will. Then we will have a beautiful baby who will be loved by me, you, and both our families."

He didn't look convinced, but he restarted the car and drove back to his flat. Sonia arrived, and Harrison headed into his home office. She wanted to ditch Sonia, follow Harrison to his desk, straddle him, and make him forget all his worries. But since the trip to the hospital, he seemed to have a no-sex rule going. It was probably for the best. It would be so much harder to leave if they still had a physical relationship. But damn, she missed his body.

At half past three, they were sitting in another waiting room. She'd filled in pages of health information, and Harrison had written a sizable amount on a check made out to the children's hospital foundation in thanks for the physician coming to the hospital on his day off.

All her test results came back normal, and the doctor cleared her to return to regular activities.

"Is it safe to return to Australia?" she asked, deliberately keeping her gaze averted from Harrison's face.

"Yes. But I recommend that you take two days to rest upon your return and have your doctor there check your blood pressure. If you leave your email address with the front desk, I'll send my report to you and you can pass it on to your obstetrician back home."

"Thank you, doctor."

The return drive took place in complete silence. She could almost see Harrison reject argument after argument in his head. He waited until they were back in his condo before he asked. "You're leaving?" His arms were crossed. Was it his tough-guy stance, or did his chest ache as badly as hers?

"Yes." Her heart shredded. It was the right answer to the wrong question.

"Why?"

She hauled in a deep breath past the weight crushing her lungs. "Because I love you, and you don't love me. If I stay any longer, I'll convince myself that it doesn't matter—that our child will be enough to hold us together. Then five years from now, I'll realize I was wrong and rip everyone's lives apart. It's better if I go now."

"No. I won't let you leave me. I won't let you take my child away." His hands were clenched in fists at his side, but she wasn't frightened. He'd never hurt her.

"Currently, there's nothing you can do. Once the baby is born, we'll come to some sort of custody arrangement. By then, I should be over you enough to think rationally." There was always a chance. They'd probably need to hire a mediator to arrive at a solution, because at the moment, standing before him, she couldn't think of one.

He reached a hand out but dropped it at his side before he touched her. "Jade, please don't do this. Give us more time. We can make this work."

God, she wanted to believe him. "Possibly. Until the day you meet someone you can love. Or I lose myself in you and can't find the way out. Trust me, it's better this way."

"I don't believe you."

"You don't have to believe me. Just drive me to the airport."

"And if I refuse?"

"I'll take a taxi."

"Jade. This isn't over."

No, she didn't think it was. But for now, she'd settle for paused.

***

Harrison looked up at the commotion coming from the outer office. It sounded like a group of protesters was about to invade. He picked up his phone to dial security. Too late, his door was flung open, but rather than an angry mob, his father, mother, sister, Caleb, and Malee strode into his office.

"Is it my birthday?" he asked as they all glared at him.

"This is an intervention," Sonia said. His eyes settled on his suitcase parked by his now-closed office door.

"I didn't realize I was on the brink of a meltdown." He was beyond the brink, in fact, and up to his hair follicles in pain. Until this moment, he thought he'd done a better job at hiding it. It had been ten days since Jade had left. He'd had one brief text message from her, saying that she'd arrived safe and was feeling fine. She'd been to the doctor and both mother and baby were doing well. End of report.

Not a second passed that he didn't wish she was closer so he could at least see for himself that she was okay. Better than okay. He wanted her to be happy. But that wasn't an option for him.

"You are about to let the best thing to ever happen to you slip away," his mother said. "We're here to make sure that you smarten up before you regret it for the rest of your life."

"If you're referring to Jade, she's the one who left me."

"You let her go," his father added.

Harrison shoved back his chair and stood. "Because otherwise, it would have been unlawful confinement." He glared at his mother. "I'm surprised you're here. You told me you didn't want me to marry her."

His mother crossed her arms and glared back at him. "That was when I thought you were with her because you felt responsible. Now that I realize you love her, it changes everything."

"She wouldn't have left if you'd told her you loved her." That sweet little gem came from Sonia.

"I won't lie to her."

"No, you'd rather lie to yourself," Caleb said. "Been there, done that, got the ring on my finger to prove I was wrong." Malcc, Caleb's wife, smiled up at her husband with such love that Harrison had to look away.

"I'm not in love with Jade." Even to his own ears, the words sounded forced.

Sonia stepped forward and banged his paperweight on his desk. "Harrison George Mackenzie, you are charged with lying to yourself about your feelings for the beautiful, kind, and loving Jade Irvine. How do you plead?"

"I'm the only lawyer in the room," he said. This farce was beyond ridiculous. He had work to do. Piles and piles of work he'd been staring at for ten days now without managing to accomplish a single thing.

"We've all watched countless TV shows about lawyers," Caleb answered. "How hard can it be?"

In the spirit of speeding this along, he'd let that jab pass … until the next time his partner asked for legal advice.

"How do you plead?" Sonia demanded.

"Not guilty."

"The Crown calls its first witness: Mrs. Lisa Patterson." He hadn't even noticed his secretary slip into the room. "Mrs. Patterson, how many phone calls have there been between the defendant and Ms. Irvine in the past three months?"

"Up until this past week, at least one a day, and that's not counting text messages," Lisa said. "His cellphone bill has gone from $120 a month to $1200."

"The woman is carrying my child. I'm concerned about her health."

Sonia ignored his perfectly logical statement. "Mrs. Patterson, how many of these phone calls and text messages occurred before Mr. Mackenzie discovered that Ms. Irvine was pregnant?"

"At least one a day. I often heard him giggling in here during the afternoon, and I knew they were texting back and forth. Or I guess the more accurate term would be *sexting*?"

"What's sexting?" his mother asked from her position on the sofa next to his father. Malee had lowered her heavily pregnant body onto a visitor's chair. Caleb stood behind her, his hands resting on, and occasionally massaging, his wife's shoulders.

Harrison was going to miss seeing Jade's belly swell with their child. Miss the feel of his baby kick and wriggle under her skin.

"Sexting is sending sexy messages and naked photos by text message," Sonia said.

His mother gasped. "Harrison, you haven't! What if the government sees them?"

"The government doesn't care about his willy," his father said. "And the girl flung off her clothes before the apartment door was even closed. Plus, she's pregnant. I think it's obvious they have a passionate relationship."

His parents were discussing his sex life now. He

was in hell.

Sonia banged the paperweight again, although from the smile on her face, she was enjoying this way too much. The girl had missed her calling; she should have gone to law school. "We're getting off topic. Mrs. Patterson, do you have anything else to add about your employer's state of mind regarding Ms. Irvine?"

"I've never seen him so happy as when she came into his life. And never as miserable as he's been since she's left."

"Thank you, Mrs. Patterson," Sonia said. "Next to give testimony, I call the defendant, Harrison Mackenzie."

He sat back down in his chair. Might as well get comfortable. This didn't seem like it was going to end anytime soon.

"So, Mr. Mackenzie…" Sonia strutted in front of his desk, exhibiting all the signs of a woman who'd watched too many legal shows on TV. "Are you happy?"

"Not at present. There are too many people in my office poking their noses into things that don't concern them."

"We love you. Your happiness is always our business," his mother said.

There was a general murmur of consent and concern. He pulled a bottle of scotch from his desk drawer and poured a generous amount straight into his coffee cup.

"It's only eleven in the morning, dear. Should you be drinking?" his mother asked. He took a hefty swallow and turned back to the assembled crowd.

"Okay, I'm not happy. I'm not going to see my child born, or get to hold him or her. I'm going to miss the first smile, first steps, everything." He took another swallow of whisky to erase the taste of bile that had risen in his throat.

"This is not about the baby. It's about Jade. Do you miss her?"

His traitorous mind flashed images of Jade's smile, of the soft glow she got in her eyes when she touched her belly, of the passion in her gaze and the flush of her skin as she climaxed with him buried deep inside her. He could almost hear the huskiness of her laugh and the sigh she released when his arms wrapped around her. She was light and joy and everything wonderful in the world. And don't get him started on her smell—the exotic flowers-and-spice combination that filled his head as he trailed his lips down her neck to the juncture of her shoulder. The scent went through his nostrils straight to his heart, where it squeezed life back into his soul. "Yes, I miss her."

Sonia leaned over the desk and stared into his eyes. "Is there something about her that you dislike enough that you don't want to be with her? Something she's lacking that you think you'd find in another woman?"

"No, she's perfect."

"Then can you explain to this group of your family and friends why the hell you think you're not in love with her? Because we can all see it, plain as day." Sonia raised her hands in the air then dropped them dramatically by her side.

"My love is toxic. Look what it did to Emily. I won't let myself love Jade."

"You are full of shit," Caleb said, loud enough to make everyone jump. "You did nothing to Emily. That girl was a snake from the start."

Harrison's stomach fell to the floor. "What do you mean?"

Caleb glanced around the room. "Maybe we should talk in private."

"No way," Sonia said. "We all have our opinions of Emily, and not many of them charitable. I don't think you'll shock anyone with what you have to say."

"What? I thought you all loved her."

"We tried for your sake, son," his father interjected. "But she was a thief and a liar long before you married her."

"How did I not know this?"

"Because when she was with you, she was sweet and lovable. I've never seen someone transform so completely. Sometimes I wondered if she were two different people." Caleb ran a hand through his hair, as if trying to decide how much to tell him. "Just as an example, while you were playing the provincial championship rugby game, she asked if we could go back to my place and have sex while you were on the field. Evidently, she'd found out how much my family was worth."

"Why did no one tell me this?" It had been sickeningly apparent that Emily had been selling her body for drugs at the end of their marriage. He'd had no idea it had been happening before.

"Because the day I went to tell you, you announced that she was pregnant and you were determined to marry her. I saw no point in bringing it up then. Besides, we all thought that once she'd captured you, she'd settle down and be happy."

"Baby Bryce was yours," his dad said from across the room. Although to Harrison, his father's voice seemed to be coming from much farther away, like thirteen years ago. "I had his DNA tested."

"Why did no one tell me this sooner?" He'd wasted years feeling guilty for not loving his wife when it appeared she'd never truly cared for him either.

Caleb answered. "You didn't even want any of us saying her name. Besides, we thought it would help if you had good memories of her."

He'd never told anyone, aside from Jade, that he'd fallen out of love with Emily long before her death. He couldn't blame them for trying to protect his memories from her true nature.

"Emily didn't deserve your love." Sonia's voice was soft, and she put her hand over his on the desk and squeezed it gently. "Jade does."

Harrison scrubbed his hands over his face. His marriage had been a lie from the start. "You've given me a lot to think about."

"You can think on the plane," Sonia said.

"Where am I going?" *Aside from insane.*

"Australia, you idiot." Sonia's smile should have

prepared him for her next words. "And we're all going with you, to make sure you don't screw up."

He glanced around the room. "All of you?" It was going to be humbling enough groveling and begging Jade to give him another chance. He didn't need his whole family watching.

"I'm staying behind, since Malee is too uncomfortable to travel that far," Caleb said. "Don't worry, I'll look after all the businesses."

"But Dad's company…"

His father stood. "We'll talk about that on the way. Come along, now. We've got a plane to catch and plans to make."

"I've always wanted to go to Australia," his mother said as she exited the room. "Do you think I'll get to play a digeridoo and pet a koala?" With the door open, Harrison could see four suitcases lined up like soldiers in a parade ground.

He was going to get his woman. With an entourage.

Chapter Twenty

The wind blew Jade's dress against her belly, revealing the tiny bump. Okay, bump was perhaps an exaggeration. She was the only one who noticed the minute change in her body. To anyone else, it probably looked like she'd had one too many pork pies. Still, she knew, and the secret lifted her lips slightly.

She dug her toes into the sand. Melbourne, with its eccentric weather, had graced them with a relatively mild winter's day, so she'd gone to the one spot where she could find a shred of peace: the beach. Getting over Harrison was proving harder than she'd thought. Out of sight was not out of mind. Not even close. Maybe because so much of their relationship had been long distance, it was hard to remember it was over before it had really begun.

A wave rushed up the beach and covered her feet in icy cold water. She stepped back before she got wetter. Getting sick now would only compound her misery.

"I'm wondering if Aussie sand has the same curative powers as Bali sand if I get it in my socks." Harrison's voice, so deep and familiar, floated over to her. Damn, now she was even hearing him in her imagination.

She turned, ready to head back to her car. Not

even the beach brought her peace of mind anymore. She glanced up ... and saw him standing in front of her.

"Harri." She couldn't believe her eyes. There he was, barefoot, with a bunch of white peonies in his hand. Further along the beach, huddled together, were his father, mother, and sister. "Shit. I'm having a stroke."

The Harrison figment of her overwrought imagination rushed to her side and wrapped his arms around her. "No stroke. Just me. I've come to beg you for another chance."

Okay, this was too good to let go. She'd let the dream take her. "A chance at what?" She closed her eyes and absorbed the warmth, the strength of the dream arms around her. His scent, so distinct yet familiar, woodsy with a hint of heat, filled her mind. *Wait.* When had she ever smelled in a dream? Even a stroke wouldn't stimulate her olfactory senses. Her eyes snapped open. "You're real?"

His lips caressed hers lightly, sparking her first real smile since she'd returned home. "I'm very real." He pressed his hips against hers, and she could feel his erection.

"How did you find me? What are you doing here?" She glanced back over her shoulder. "What is your family doing here?"

"Your father said if you weren't at home, I should try this beach. And I'm here to tell you I love you." He nodded toward his family. "They're here to make sure I don't screw it up."

Butterflies in her stomach took off, but she ruthlessly pushed them back into their cage. "What makes you think you love me?"

"Let's see… I can't eat or sleep because I miss you. I haven't done a lick of work since you left. I compare everything to you. Do you know how many shades of green there are in the world? And that none are as beautiful as your eyes?"

"You like my eye color?"

"I love it. Where was I? Oh, yes, I think about you constantly. I want to see you smile more than I want to breathe. Basically, I'm a basket case without you. So, I've come to ask if there is any way, in any capacity, you'll allow me back into your life."

"I always said I'd grant you access to our child."

"I'm not talking about our child's life. I want to be part of *your* life. Ideally, I want to be your husband, your lover, your protector, your confidante, occasionally the guy who makes you laugh so hard you pee yourself a bit, but always the man who loves you unconditionally."

The butterflies were free. Her heart went with them. "Well, it just so happens that I have such an opening."

"Does that mean you'll marry me?" He sank down on one knee, the wet sand quickly soaking through his trousers. He handed her the flowers then held out a velvet box. She opened it with shaking hands. Nestled inside was a solitaire oval emerald surrounded by diamonds. "See what I mean? Endless shades of green." The hint of nervousness in his voice convinced her of his sincerity. He'd always been so sure of himself.

"Yes, I'll marry you."

He rose and pulled her tight against him, crushing the poor peonies between them. "Thank God." His kiss was full of love and relief. When he finally raised his head, he called out, "She said yes. You can get lost now."

A loud cheer went up behind him.

"You can't tell your family to get lost."

"I can, and I did. I want all of you, preferably naked, to myself for at least twelve hours."

"I like the naked bit, provided you reciprocate."

"Most definitely." The heat in his smile went straight to her core. He grabbed her hand and headed up the beach. "We're on the clock. My hotel or your apartment?"

"What do mean, we're on the clock?" She stopped walking and waited for him to turn around.

"We have a flight to catch tomorrow at two. We're flying to Bali, where we're getting married."

Some things did not change. "Hold up. Two minutes ago, you asked me to marry you, and now you tell me you've got it all arranged?"

He had the sense to look sheepish. "Not all of it. You get to choose the actual location. We could have it on the beach where we had dinner the first night, the mini island where we had dinner and slept in the hammock, the ruins you took me to, or my personal favorite, the back deck of your house. Although that last one might be crowded with both our families."

"Our families are coming?"

"And Karly and Hugh, Jules, and Lauren, and their boyfriends."

"So you just assumed I'd say yes and went and organized everything?"

"My contingencies have contingencies, remember. And I didn't plan everything—I delegated. Sonia and her designer friend Mandy sorted out the dresses. Lauren, Karly, and Jules took care of the rest of the wedding plans, and our parents have been sticking their noses into everything, giving unsolicited advice."

She pulled her hand out of his and crossed her arms. "I don't like being told what to do."

"Except in the bedroom."

"Well, there is that."

He unwrapped her arms and pulled her back into his. "Tell you what… After this, we will make all major life decisions together. But I can't wait to make you my wife, and it takes a month here in Australia to get a marriage license."

"That's to stop people from rushing blindly into things."

"We're not blind. I've finally had my eyes opened. I love you. Only you. Even if you weren't having my baby, which you are, I'd still want to marry you. And once a businessman makes a decision, he acts on it."

"I've gone from being a responsibility to a business decision. Maybe this is a mistake, Harri." She pulled away again, but only so she could see his face.

Her heart, her body, wanted to throw herself at him and damn the consequences. The one tiny part of her not intoxicated by his presence reminded her that this discussion would form the basis for the rest of their lives together. If she wanted any power in their relationship, she had to hold firm now.

He put his hands on her hips and drew her lower half against his body. His lips were warm on her ear as he traced the shape with his tongue. "Have I told you how much I love it when you call me Harri? Makes me hard just hearing it."

"You're trying to change the subject." Her head dropped back as his lips trailed down her neck. She hoped his parents and sister were gone, not to mention anyone else on the beach, because she couldn't guarantee that her clothes were going to stay on much longer.

"Is it working?" His tongue traced her collarbone.

"Damn you, Harrison Mackenzie, you're not listening to me."

He finally raised his head, but his eyes were anything but remorseful. "I'm going to hear that a lot, aren't I?"

"You are when you steamroll over my wishes."

"What are your wishes?"

"Um…" Ten minutes ago, she'd have been happy to forget he existed.

"Do you want to marry me?"

"Yes."

"Do you want to do it sooner or later? Bear in mind that you're already in your second trimester."

"Sooner. But I haven't got a dress or anything."

"Lauren and Sonia have that in hand. I believe they have twenty dresses for you to choose from tomorrow morning, all in your size. And a seamstress is on hand to make any alterations required."

"And after the whirlwind wedding? Are we going back to Canada to live in that house on the beach?"

"That, my love, is entirely up to you."

She raised an eyebrow. "I thought you had to stay in Canada to run your father's company."

"He's selling it."

"What? Wasn't it supposed to be his legacy?"

"He said he started the company to provide for his family. Now it's tearing the family apart. He'd rather his legacy was love."

A tear slid down her cheek. "Oh my God, that's so beautiful."

"Not as beautiful as you. Jade, you are my life. You are my family now, my priority. Even if Dad wasn't selling, I would still move here if this is where you want to be."

"There are no mountains."

"You said you wanted a love that moved mountains. How about a love that no longer requires them? If I have you, I need nothing else."

The tears fell in a torrent now. "Damn pregnancy hormones."

"I like the hormones. You are more beautiful every time I see you. Is that a baby bump I'm feeling?"

"Just a tiny one."

"It'll get big. Until then, I'm going to hold you

close every chance I get."

She pulled his head down for a scorching kiss. She had his love, and there was nothing else she needed. Except…

"I have one last question," Jade said when they finally came up for air.

"And that is?" He wrapped an arm around her waist and steered her toward the car park.

"How much time do we have in Bali before the wedding is to take place?"

"Two days or so. We have some paperwork to take care of. Why?"

"Because I think we should put durian fruit in the offices of those crooked T-shirt manufacturers to let them know they're giving my motherland a bad name."

He stopped walking and blinked twice. Then a radiant smile lifted his lips. "If it will give you peace of mind, I'm game."

"What? I thought you'd try to talk, or kiss me, out of my misadventures."

"Sometimes I will. But Granny Celia told me that you were Karly's savior. You're mine as well. So it would be counterproductive to curb all of your miraculous healing powers, mischievous antics included."

"I'm so glad you realize that already."

"I'm a smart man."

Her laugh floated away on the ocean breeze. It didn't matter. There'd be plenty more where that one came from.

Epilogue

One year later

Harrison gently took his almost-sleeping daughter from Jade. The baby opened her bright blue eyes briefly, as if to see who was holding her now. A contented smile curved her chubby cheeks before she closed her eyes again and snuggled against his neck. His chest flooded with warmth. At this moment, he didn't think it was possible to be any happier.

Jade refastened her bra and sent him an indulgent smile. "Are you sure you want to go out tonight? I don't mind staying in."

He rubbed baby Ruby's back to help bring up any air she'd swallowed while nursing. Hopefully, that's all she'd produce—he'd forgotten to put a spit cloth over his shoulder and he was already dressed for dinner. Although it wouldn't be the first time he'd gone out with baby puke on him. And he wouldn't have it any other way.

"We're eating out on our first wedding anniversary. My parents and Sonia are here to look after Ruby, and we'll only be gone a couple hours." He said it aloud to reassure himself. It was still difficult for him to leave the baby with others. Although, at eight months old, Ruby was past the greatest risk stage for SIDS, it still lingered in the back of his mind. "Besides, I thought you couldn't wait to get reacquainted with Bali sand."

"All right, then. I'll get dressed." Jade dropped a kiss on their baby's little hand resting over his heart before going into the bedroom.

"Hand over my niece, brother," Sonia said as she walked across the room. "I know you. You'll sit down and let Ruby fall asleep on your chest, and then you'll never leave."

It was true. The first three months of Ruby's life had mostly been spent in his arms. "I'm just burping her," he said, but he handed the precious bundle over to his sister. Ruby gave a soft cry of disappointment that wrung the blood from his heart. But she quickly settled into her aunt's arms.

Sonia rubbed Ruby's back while doing a little bounce motion. "While Jade's out of the room, I wanted to ask… What's the story with your new business partner?"

Harrison narrowed his eyes. "Ethan? Why? And why did you have to wait until Jade left to ask?"

"Because I heard her muttering something about 'fixing him.' I can't see anything wrong and wondered what she was on about."

"Stay away from Ethan. He's brilliant in business but ruthless. Guys don't get like that without some sort of baggage."

"More than you had before you met Jade?"

That startled a smile from him. "Probably not. But I don't want my sister dating my business partner, baggage or no baggage."

"I wasn't asking for me. Mandy saw him and was interested."

Likely story. But before he could grill his sister further, Jade strolled out of the bedroom wearing only a robe, her nipples clearly outlined through the silky material.

"Before I try and squeeze myself into a pre-pregnancy dress, I wanted to make sure you haven't changed your mind about going out." She put her hands on her hips, and the lapels of her robe pulled apart, revealing the deep valley between her breasts. Maybe staying in would be best. They could get room service and remain in close proximity to a bed … shower … wall…

Sonia issued a disgusting snort. Obviously his face had given away his thoughts. "Take Jade out. Mom and I will look after Ruby tonight, and you can get started on a little brother or sister for her."

Conflicting emotions ripped through him. Once the initial fear of miscarriage had passed, Jade had loved being pregnant and began pestering him to have another baby right away. But he wasn't sure his heart could take the constant worry. He was only just beginning to relax about leaving Ruby with his family.

"Why don't you meet me in the bar?" Jade said. "Then, if you change your mind, we're not too far away to return."

He kissed Jade lightly on the mouth. "I won't

change my mind, but thanks for giving me the option." God, he loved this woman. He needed to suck up his worries and show her how much she meant to him.

As he sipped a whisky in the hotel bar downstairs, waiting for Jade, he formed a plan for the next day. The most important thing would be to take Ruby to the beach so she could get her first feel of Bali sand between her toes. After that, they'd leave her in the care of her grandparents and aunt, and he and Jade could head up to the rice terrace house for a few hours. With any luck, there might even be a rain shower they could mutually enjoy. His blood heated as his mind produced the image of soap suds sliding down Jade's naked body. Even after a year of marriage, she could arouse him with just a lift of her eyebrows.

This was their first trip back to Bali since their wedding. Despite being hastily put together, Jade had declared it to be everything she'd ever wanted. She'd stood by his side, on the beach, with her family and friends, looking so beautiful he thought his chest would burst from happiness.

Following an all-too-brief honeymoon spent at Caleb and Malee's holiday home in northern Thailand, they'd moved into the house in Point Grey. Harrison had had to help his father get his company ready to sell and had aided in the transition. The final transaction had taken place last week, so the family were all holidaying in Indonesia for a week before Jade, Ruby, and Harrison went to Australia for a month.

Jade was excited to introduce their daughter to Karly and Hugh's son, Jacob. And of course, attend their friend Jules's wedding. The poor bride... She'd had to delay her nuptials because two of her closest friends had insisted they have some time to lose the extra weight they'd put on during their pregnancies first.

"Hey, son, what are you doing here alone?" His father rested his large frame on the stool next to Harrison's. The last year had been hard on his dad, with his health issues and worry over his company. But now that it was all settled, the light had come back into his eyes and a weight seemed to have lifted from his shoulders. Hamish was going to keep busy as an adviser to Sonia in her fashion business, which despite Harrison's initial worries, seemed to be taking off.

"Jade is getting ready, and Sonia's looking after the baby while we go for dinner. Where's Mom?"

"You know your mother; she won't relax until she's unpacked. Evidently, I was getting in her way. I expect I'll be hearing that a lot..."

Whatever else his Dad said became white noise as Jade strolled into the bar. She'd put on the same dress she'd worn the first night they'd met. The one that made him want to rip it off her body and take her right there on the bar. If she was commando underneath, they weren't going to make it out of the hotel.

His father's chuckle broke through the lust that had engulfed Harrison at the sight of his wife in *that* dress. "I'll go drag Sue away from her unpacking. Happy anniversary, son. I can't tell you how relieved your mother and I are to see you enjoy life again. I am so proud of you and your beautiful family."

"Thanks, Dad."

Hamish said something to Jade as they passed, and she kissed his father on the cheek before making her way over to the now-vacant stool next to him.

"Are you waiting for your wife or girlfriend?" she asked.

"My wife. Maybe you've seen her—she's the most beautiful woman in the world and makes me happier than I ever thought possible."

"Sounds like a great woman."

"She's perfect." He cupped her cheek and traced her full lips with his thumb. "Thank you for the best year of my life."

"Right back at ya," she replied with a husky catch in her voice.

"Are you wearing anything under that dress?"

Her sexy laugh shot heat straight to his groin. "You'll have to wait to find out."

"You are a wicked woman, Jade Irvine-Mackenzie." He finished his whisky then escorted her from the bar to the hotel restaurant. It seemed the perfect compromise—they were out, but not too far away in case Ruby wouldn't settle.

"Wicked? I thought you said I was perfect." She tilted her face up to him and his heart did its now-familiar flutter.

"You are. I wouldn't change a thing about you." His lips met hers in a kiss of tenderness that promised passion once they were alone.

After the waiter took their order, he took Jade's hand in his, twirling her wedding and engagement ring. "I'm thinking of having Ruby's name and date of birth tattooed on my arm under Bryce's. I don't want her to think I love her less."

Jade's laugh lifted his own lips. "Oh, petal, you lavish so much love on her that there's no way she would ever doubt your devotion. But if that's what you want, just make sure you leave enough room for the rest of our children."

"There's going to be that many?"

She let go of his hand and inched up his arm, tracing Bryce's name with her index finger. "Yup. You know you can't resist me. And when I want something…"

"I'm putty in your hands."

Her fingers slid up to his biceps, and his skin heated under her touch. "You don't feel like putty to me. But while you're at the tattoo parlor, I may join you. My ink needs some correction. Love isn't an illusion. It's real and more wonderful than I ever imagined. I love you, Harri, with everything I am."

"Everything you are is exquisite. I am the most fortunate man alive to have you as my wife."

Her smile rivaled the sun for brilliance. "Yes, you are. And I will never let you forget it."

He kissed the back of her hand. Bali may have brought him back to life, but Jade made it worth living.

****

Thank you for reading *Bali with the Billionaire*. Please post a review where you purchased the book. Your opinion will not only help other readers decide whether to buy the book or not, it will also help me continue to write the stories that I, and hopefully you, love to read. Thank you!

Have you read my Vintage Love series?

(PS. It's not about old love, it's about love in the vineyards.)

The Vintner and The Vixen

It's all fun and games until someone falls in love.

Maya Tessier needs a fresh start after her last boyfriend dragged her deep into an organized crime ring, putting her life in danger. After inheriting a cottage and acreage in France from her great-grandmother, she hopes to escape her turbulent past to concentrate on her art. Unfortunately, her inheritance is within the estate of a privacy-obsessed billionaire. And he wants it all back.

Jacques de Launay has led a life of rigid control, working hard to repair the family's fortunes after his playboy father nearly destroyed them. His one attempt at happiness ended in tragedy when his pregnant wife was killed in a car crash. He'd rather be the last in the illustrious de Launay family line than open himself up to that kind of heartache again. Then Maya Tessier arrives on his doorstep and he discovers it's not only the ancestral land he wants to reclaim.

But if he lets her stay, more than his heart may be at risk.

The Vintner and The Vixen

Chapter One

Jacques raked a hand through his hair then immediately pulled a comb out of his pocket and straightened the strands. *Merci Dieu* it was Friday and he could escape from Paris to the Loire Valley. Except there he'd have to endure an entire weekend listening to his grandfather ask when he was going to marry again and continue the family name. Jacques was pretty sure his grandfather was still alive at ninety-five because he didn't trust his grandson to procreate without his continual reminders.

His phone buzzed on his desk seconds before his secretary's voice came over the intercom, starting with a giggle.

"Jacques, your grandfather is on line one, and he sounds very excited. And your brother is here—" Another giggle. Was there any woman his brother couldn't charm? Even Jacques's fifty-five-year-old, married-for-decades personal assistant was reduced to a schoolgirl when Daniel showed up.

"Send in Daniel; I'll take the call."

His younger brother strode through the door as Jacques picked up the handset. His granddad hated being on speakerphone.

"She's come," Grand-Papa said without greeting.

"Who's come?" Jacques rolled his eyes at Daniel, who lounged on the chair in front of the desk. His brother wore jeans and a white shirt with the top three buttons undone. And if Jacques wasn't mistaken, and he never was, a woman's lipstick mark was under the curve of his brother's jaw. Must be nice to indulge in lovemaking in the middle of a workday. Or any day for that matter. But Daniel had never had a problem attracting the ladies. Remembering where he'd left them was another story.

"Yvette." His grandfather's voice saved him from contemplating his brother's love life. At least he had one.

"What?" He stood, and even Daniel sat up in his chair. "Grand-Papa, Daniel's here. I'm going to put you on speakerphone so we both can hear your news." He pressed the button on the phone but didn't sit back down. "Now, start at the beginning. Who has arrived?"

Jacques had been expecting this for a while, but his grandfather's mind suddenly snapping was still a shock.

"Yvette. Or rather, her great-granddaughter."

"What?" He was beginning to sound like a parrot.

"Yvette has passed and left the cottage and land to her great-granddaughter. She's come to claim it." His grandfather's voice softened as though he were explaining a difficult concept to a child.

Jacques fell into his chair. "Where is this woman now?"

"I don't think this phone is working. Or else you're not listening. I just said she's at the cottage. You are still coming home tonight, right?"

Jacques counted to ten, then backwards for good measure. "Grand-Papa, are you saying that some girl showed up, claiming to be the great-granddaughter of a woman you haven't seen in more than seventy years, and you just let her move into the cottage?"

"Yes."

Daniel put his hand over his mouth to cover a laugh. Jacques glared at him. Didn't he realize how serious this was? Not only had a complete stranger moved into a building on their property, but she might also hold the title deed to their very best grapevines. Jacques sent an IM to his secretary, asking her to get his lawyer on the line.

"Did she have proof of ownership?"

"I don't need proof. She has Yvette's eyes."

Jacques didn't even try to stifle the groan that rose in his throat. "So, to recap, you met someone who has the same eye color as a woman you knew before 'La Vie en rose' was a hit? And that entitled this stranger to invade our estate?"

"She had a key."

Oh. That makes it all right, then.

"I'm on my way." Jacques disconnected the call and checked his watch. The next TGV train didn't depart for an hour, but the drive took two and a half—plenty of time for the thief to make off with all the antiques in the cottage. His grandfather had insisted the place remain exactly as it had been when he'd gifted it to Yvette during the Second World War. By allowing his grandfather to maintain the cottage and keep it move-in ready, Jacques had precipitated this entire event.

The only thing he could do now was get down there quickly, get rid of this woman, and make sure his grandfather had someone to keep a closer eye on him.

Jacques shoved his laptop and some papers in his briefcase.

"I've got a company car. I'll drive," Daniel said.

Jacques paused. "You know I don't like being driven."

"You want to get there today, don't you? You drive like an old lady on her way to church on Sunday."

"I drive the speed limit. Not everyone is a Formula 1 driver."

"Gotta be the best to do what I do. Jacques, if Mercedes trusts me to drive their 2.5-million-euro car, you should trust me to drive you home. Come on. I, for one, can't wait to meet this woman with the unforgettable eyes."

"Of course you can't."

As they left, Jacques's secretary transferred the lawyer through to his cell phone. But they'd already had this conversation. The property legally belonged to Yvette Tessier and formed part of her estate. The only way the de Launay family could reclaim the land was to buy it back. Maybe he should get Daniel to approach this woman on the off chance it was a relative who wanted to liquidate her assets—or had no idea what they were worth. His brother could probably get the Queen of England to sell Windsor Castle to him.

Jacques deliberately kept his eyes off the speedometer as Daniel drove. His brother made his living driving very powerful cars very, very fast. But even though he had full confidence in Daniel's ability to get them home safely, giving up control didn't sit easy with Jacques.

Daniel slowed as they wound their way through the village near the chateau. A black motorbike followed behind, inches from their back bumper. As soon as the road straightened, the bike flew by, the rider giving a jaunty wave. The scream of the engine gave even Jacques a minor thrill. Daniel sped up to keep the bike—or maybe the rider's amazing ass—in view. The biker looked back over her shoulder and then, with a burst of speed, disappeared.

They pulled into the drive just as the gates clanged closed. Someone had entered just before their arrival.

Please don't let the biker be Yvette's great-granddaughter.

"Do you want to go to the house or cottage first?" Daniel asked.

"I'll go to the cottage first, see what we're dealing with. You go to the house and check on Grand-Papa. We're going to have to talk about hiring a companion to keep an eye on him. All this being alone isn't good."

"Aye, aye, Captain."

Jacques shot him a withering glare, which just bounced off his brother's good humor. The only time Daniel was ever serious was when he was on the racetrack.

Sure enough, a black Ducati motorbike was parked beside the cottage. Just what he needed, a biker chick to deal with. He straightened his tie and was about to knock on the door when it opened.

Mon Dieu.

Her riding leathers were unzipped to her waist. A tiny, black crop top barely covered full breasts, and an expanse of creamy white skin disappeared beyond the zipper. But it was her halo of fiery red hair that caught his eye. It fell with abandon about her face and down her back, a single curl resting against her cleavage. She came with her own sunset.

"I thought I heard someone. You must be Charles's grandson—Jacques de Launay, isn't it?"

Damned if her voice didn't match her body, sultry and sumptuous. Her French had a Canadian accent but was perfectly understandable.

He cleared his throat. "You have me at a disadvantage. You obviously know who I am."

"And I bet you hate that, don't you?"

"Hate what?"

"That I know more about you than you do about me." She cocked a hand on her hip and the zipper pulled apart another couple centimeters, revealing more alabaster skin. Strawberries and cream. His mouth watered.

"It's not my favorite position to be in," he said.

A delighted laugh escaped her full lips. They were devoid of sticky lip gunk, perfect for kissing. He dragged his gaze from her mouth back to her smiling eyes.

"Perhaps before we discuss favorite positions, I should at least tell you my name. I'm Maya Tessier."

Her handshake was firm, and the laughter in her eyes never wavered. Jacques forced his lips to remain neutral. He wouldn't be beguiled by this woman's flirtatious attitude.

"What do you want, Ms. Tessier?"

"Call me Maya. After all, we're neighbors now."

"Over my dead body."

Her eyes raked him. "That would be a horrific waste of what appears to be a mighty fine body." This time his smile wouldn't be repressed. The women he normally associated with weren't like this—bold, brash, and hot enough to scorch the inside of an oak barrel.

The last thing he needed was to repeat his grandfather's folly and be suckered by a woman he'd never get over. *Not going to happen. Refocus, Jacques. She's just a woman out to get what she can from the family. Like all the others.*

He'd make quick work of this and get back to his relaxing weekend. Her gaze was riveted on his lips. She licked her own, and the air between them sizzled.

To hell with relaxation. Maya was a challenge he wasn't about to ignore.

***

What was it about authority that brought out the sass in her? The man before her reeked of power. Tightly controlled, highly suppressed power. Not a hair was out of place, his suit probably cost more than her bike, and despite having walked across the dusty gravel, not a speck had dared settle on his polished shoes. The whole package made her want to rumple him until he never looked pressed again.

It would be no hardship either. The man was seriously gorgeous. His eyes were the same blue as his grandfather's, his hair light brown but highlighted with blond as though he spent a lot of time outside rather than behind a desk. Either that or he had a fabulous colorist. The thought of the powerful Jacques de Launay with aluminum foil in his hair nearly set off a fit of the giggles. His full lips tightened as he continued to stare at her. Yup, authority brought out her rebellious streak. And usually got her in deep trouble. Chances were, she was heading that way now. Trouble in the guise of a sexy Frenchman.

Yes, please.

Her internal temperature went critical, and she pulled off her riding leathers to cool down. Jacques's eyes flared as he watched her undress.

"So ... Maya, I imagine you are anxious to get rid of the property and return to Canada and your family." He still stood in the doorway, his head almost reaching the lintel, his shoulders nearly spanning the width. Her body hummed, but not from fear. She'd been around enough men to know which ones resorted to their fists to exert strength over a woman. Jacques would probably just kiss her into submission. *Get a grip, Maya. He's here to wheedle your inheritance out of you.* Her best plan was to knock him off balance.

"Such a vivid imagination. Surely, it could be put to better use. But to answer your question, no, I'm here to stay. Lucky for me, my father is Irish and I have the right to live in Europe. So, as I said, we're now neighbors."

"I would make you a very generous offer for the cottage and land. You could get a nice place in Paris. Surely a woman like you wants to live in the city, not be stuck out here in the countryside."

"A woman like me? Since you've known me all of two minutes, perhaps you'd like to elaborate on exactly what type of woman you think I am."

His gaze caressed her again. "You are young, beautiful, and according to your left hand, single. Paris has clubs, restaurants, shops, everything to keep you amused. I would pay you 10 million euros, and I can advise you on how to invest it so you'd never have to work again."

"That is a generous offer. However, my clubbing days are over. I prefer to eat at home. And as you can see from my wardrobe"—she gestured to her department store jeans and cotton top—"my taste in clothes is simple. Let me make myself clear, *Monsieur* de Launay. I am here to stay. Now, if you'll excuse me, I have a dinner date in half an hour and need to dress." She grabbed the door and, barely giving him time to step back, slammed it in his face.

That went well. At least it'd been the reaction

she'd expected from Jacques—to try and get her off his estate right away. She had to calm down before she pitched up at his table in a few minutes. Awkward family dinners were nothing new for her. She looked forward to seeing how Jacques de Launay handled them.

Get your copy of The Vintner and The Vixen now!

Thank you, reader

I hope you enjoyed reading Harrison and Jade's story as much as I enjoyed writing it. If you did, **please, please** help others find it by leaving a **review** at your favorite retailer. Your review doesn't have to be long, but your opinion matters to me and other readers.

Want to be one of the first to know about upcoming releases, contests, and events? Sign up for my monthly newsletter at https://alexia-adams.com.

You can also chat with me on Facebook (https://www.facebook.com/AlexiaAdamsAuthor) and Twitter (@AlexiaAdamsAuth) or, of course, get in touch with me via my website (https://alexia-adams.com).

I love to hear from readers, so don't be shy.

About the Author

Alexia Adams was born in British Columbia, Canada, and traveled throughout North America as a child. After high school, she spent three months in Panama before moving to Dunedin, New Zealand, for a year, where she studied French and Russian at Otago University.

Back in Canada, she worked building fire engines until she'd saved enough for a round-the-world ticket. She traveled throughout Australasia before settling in London—the perfect place to indulge her love of history and travel. For four years, she lived and traveled throughout Europe before returning to her homeland. On the way back to Canada she stopped in Egypt, Jordan, Israel, India, Nepal, and of course, Australia and New Zealand. She lived again in Canada for one year before the lure of Europe and easy travel was too great, and she returned to the UK.

Marriage and the birth of two babies later, she moved back to Canada to raise her children with her British husband. Two more children were born in Canada, and her travel wings were well and truly clipped. Firmly rooted in the life of a stay-at-home mom, or trophy wife, as she prefers to be called, she turned to writing to exercise her mind, traveling vicariously through her romance novels.

Her stories reflect her love of travel and feature locations as diverse as the windswept prairies of Canada to hot and humid cities in Asia. To discover other books written by Alexia or read her blog on inspirational destinations, visit her at https://Alexia-Adams.com or follow her on Twitter @AlexiaAdamsAuth

Other Books by Alexia:

Love in Translation series:

Thailand with the Tycoon

Will being trapped in a failing resort change more than their itinerary? When his older brother suffers a heart-attack, Caleb is sucked back into the family's virtually bankrupt business. He reluctantly travels to Thailand to evaluate a last-chance resort with the help of a translator. Getting stranded with an enchanting local was not on the agenda. Neither was falling in love.

To read an excerpt visit my website:
Alexia-adams.com

Vintage Love series:

The Vintner and The Vixen

After witnessing a murder, Maya Tessier needs to disappear. So she escapes to the cottage in France she inherited from her great-grandmother where she hopes to start a new life and concentrate on her art. Jacques de Launay doesn't like strangers on his estate, especially when they're a sexy redhead who reminds him of all he's lost. But if he lets her stay, more than his heart may be at risk.

To read an excerpt visit my website:
Alexia-adams.com

The Playboy and The Single Mum

Single mother Lexy Camparelli must accompany super sexy Formula 1 driver Daniel Michaud for the rest of the race season as part of her job. Will she be able to keep her life on track and her heart from crashing or will the stress of living in the spotlight bring back her eating disorder or worse, jeopardize custody of her son?

To read an excerpt visit my website:
Alexia-adams.com

The Tycoon and The Teacher

Argentinian tycoon Santiago Alvarez will do whatever it takes to keep custody of his niece Miranda—even if it means marriage to the woman who jeopardizes his peace of mind. Genevieve Dubois is finding her way again after a traumatic experience left her unable to teach in a classroom. Helping an eight-year-old girl come to terms with the loss of her parents is challenge enough without the continual distracting presence of the sexy uncle who refuses to love. Then she discovers the real reason Santiago wants to retain guardianship of Miranda and it threatens all their futures.

To read an excerpt visit my website:
Alexia-adams.com

The Developer and The Diva

Para siempre means forever. That's what they'd promised one another. Then she left. Now she's back, and para siempre is just two words written on the wall of the community center he's determined to tear down … and she wants to save. Will the pain of the past be too much to overcome, or will they gamble again on a love to last para siempre?

To read an excerpt visit my website:
Alexia-adams.com

Guide to Love series:

Miss Guided

Mystery writer Marcus Sullivan is determined find someone for his younger brother Liam. Playing matchmaker on holiday in St. Lucia, Marcus tries to interest Liam in beautiful local tour guide Crescentia St. Ives. Then Marcus gets stranded with Crescentia and the plot to match her with his brother quickly incinerates in the flames of lust. No way can Liam have her when Marcus can't keep his hands off. Too bad he can't write a happier ending to their blossoming romance.

To read an excerpt visit my website:
Alexia-adams.com

Played by the Billionaire

Internet security billionaire, Liam Manning, made a promise to his beloved brother, Marcus, to complete his mystery-romance manuscript. Problem is that Liam's experience with women is limited to the cold-hearted supermodels he usually dates. So falling back on his hacking skills, he infiltrates an online dating site to find a suitable woman to teach him about romance—regular guy style. What he didn't expect was for the feelings to be so…real. Can Liam finish the novel before Lorelei discovers his deceptions and, more critically, before she breaches the firewall around his heart?

To read an excerpt visit my website:
Alexia-adams.com

His Billion-Dollar Dilemma

Simon Lamont is an ice-cold corporate pirate. But when he arrives in San Francisco to acquire a floundering company and is accosted by a cute engineer with fire in her eyes, it takes all Simon has to maintain his legendary cool. Helen will do whatever it takes to change his mind, and if that means becoming the sexy woman Simon didn't know he wanted, so be it. If only she wasn't about to walk into her own trap...

To read an excerpt visit my website:
Alexia-adams.com

Masquerading with the Billionaire

World-renowned jewelry designer Remington Wolfe is competing for the commission of a lifetime and someone is trying to destroy his company from the inside. He's in for more than one surprise when his unexpected rescuer turns out to be a sexy computer specialist with a sharp tongue and even sharper mind.

To read an excerpt visit my website:

Alexia-adams.com

Romance and Intrigue in the Greek Islands:

The Greek's Stowaway Bride

Hoping to make it to North Africa to free her uncle, Rania Ghalli stows away on the yacht of Greek millionaire Demetri Christodoulou. But when Egyptian agents board the boat, she can either jump overboard…or claim she's Demetri's new bride. Demetri needs a wife to complete a land purchase so he agrees to play along—if she'll agree to a real marriage. But keeping the vivacious woman out of his heart will be a lot harder than keeping her on his ship…

To read an excerpt visit my website:

Alexia-adams.com

An Inconvenient Series:

An Inconvenient Love

With the Italian economy in ruins, Luca Castellioni can't afford a distraction from running his successful property restoration company. However, he needs an English-speaking wife to cement a crucial deal. When his British bride-of-convenience undermines the foundations around his heart, he's forced to restructure his priorities. Is he too late for love?

To read an excerpt visit my website:
Alexia-adams.com

An Inconvenient Desire

Investment banker Jonathan Davis retreats to his Italian villa to lick his wounds post divorce, so his flirtation with runway model Olivia Chapman is just that. But when his ex dumps their toddler daughter on his doorstep, Olivia's assistance is a godsend that shakes up his world in more ways than one.

To read an excerpt visit my website:
Alexia-adams.com

Daring to Love Again Series:

The Sicilian's Forgotten Wife

Bella Vanni has accepted that her presumed-dead husband is long gone, so it's a huge shock when he knocks on her door and announces his desire to resume their marriage. She can't trust his answers on where he's been or why he left, and she certainly isn't keen to walk away from the life she's constructed for herself in his absence. But when Matteo's freedom is threatened, Bella must decide which is most important to her: everything she's painstakingly built or a second chance at a love that never died.

To read an excerpt visit my website:
Alexia-adams.com

Romance in the Canadian Prairie:

Her Faux Fiancé

Take one fake engagement to a man she once loved, stir in a very real pregnancy, add a marriage of convenience, and bake in the heat of revenge, and you get the mess that has become Analise's life.

To read an excerpt visit my website:
Alexia-adams.com

Business Trip Romance:

Singapore Fling

Lalita Evans's father hired Jeremy Lakewood in the family's international conglomerate, and now he's tagging along as she oversees their interests across eight countries in three weeks. Will Jeremy risk his livelihood and all the success he's achieved to win the woman who haunts his dreams?

To read an excerpt visit my website:
Alexia-adams.com

Manufactured by Amazon.ca
Bolton, ON